I0450930

FAE WITCH'S VAMPIRE GUARD
Dark Lords of London
Book 3

JESSIE DONOVAN

Mythical Lake Press, LLC

Fae Witch's Vampire Guard

Copyright © 2022 Laura Hoak-Kagey

Mythical Lake Press, LLC

Print Edition

Cover Art by Laura Hoak-Kagey of Mythical Lake Design

ISBN: 9781944776558

Also by Jessie Donovan

Dark Lords of London

Vampire's Modern Bride (DLL #1)

Vampire's Fae Witch Healer (DLL #2)

Fae Witch's Vampire Guard (DLL #3)

Vampires' Shared Bride (DLL #4 / Early 2026)

Wolf's Fae Witch Lord / Grace & Kahn (DLL #5 / 2026)

Dragon Clan Gatherings

Summer at Lochguard (DCG #1)

Winter at Stonefire (DCG #2)

Kelderan Runic Warriors

The Conquest (KRW #1)

The Barren (KRW #2)

The Heir (KRW #3)

The Forbidden (KRW #4)

The Hidden (KRW #5)

The Survivor (KRW #6)

Lochguard Highland Dragons

The Dragon's Dilemma (LHD #1)

The Dragon Guardian (LHD #2)

Frozen Desires (AMT #2)

Shadow of Temptation (AMT #3)

Flare of Promise (AMT #4)

Cascade Shifters

Convincing the Cougar (CS #0.5)

Reclaiming the Wolf (CS #1)

Cougar's First Christmas (CS #2)

Resisting the Cougar (CS #3)

Love in Scotland

Crazy Scottish Love (LiS #1)

Chaotic Scottish Wedding (LiS #2)

WRITING AS KAYLA CHASE

(Sexy contemporary romances)

Starry Hills

Want Me Forever

Stay With Me Forever

Marry Me Forever

Trust Me With Forever

A Note About Terms

The majority of this book takes place in 1890, and as a result, some of the words or phrases we use every day in the twenty-first century will be different in the past. Please be aware that using those different terms was done deliberately. (I.e. gaming hell is the phrase that means casino, etc.) I always make it clear through context what those older terms/phrases mean, though. Besides, part of the fun of this series is having future versus past constantly battling it out with one another. I hope you enjoy reading it as much as I did writing it. — JD

Chapter One

July 2003
Vancouver, BC, Canada

R eika Hashimoto finished locking up the bakery where she worked and headed down the street, toward the waterfront and the nearby Pacific Spirit Park. Thanks to it being summer and the sun not going down until late, she loved going for a walk after work. It gave her time to brainstorm and organize her ideas and projects—or even think about her dream of opening a restaurant one day—before she had to catch the bus back home.

For the most part, she didn't mind working at the bakery. Since she was half fae witch and half shifter, she had magic and could improve the taste of anything organic with her powers.

Working with food and cooking in any capacity made her happy. And since her boss was her stepdad's friend, he'd given her a chance and left her mostly in charge of the menu.

But even if she'd learned a lot about the day-to-day operations of a food-related business, it was a far cry from being able to run her own place and be the boss. Her dream was to rent a building where she could put a bakery on one side—which offered both Canadian favorites and those she missed from Japan—and on the other? A restaurant that also blended the cuisine of her two homes.

Quite the ambition for someone only twenty-five years old, but Reika was close, so close, to being able to start putting her plans into action. After maybe one more year of saving she could start with a small bakery of her own, finally taking a step toward her bigger dreams.

If only obaa-chan were still alive. Even though she'd moved to Canada at age ten, when her mother had remarried to a Canadian shifter, Reika had spent every New Year's with her paternal grandmother in Japan. Well, at least until she'd passed away a few years ago. The days of them making *osechi ryōri*—special New Year's dishes—were still some of her favorite memories. It was because of her grandmother that Reika had learned to love cooking in the first place, years before discovering her magical abilities.

She hadn't returned to her old hometown of Otsu since her grandmother's death, though. It was simply too painful. Especially since her dad had died when she'd been eight. And her mother's family hadn't approved of their fae witch daughter marrying an Asian bear shifter, to the point Reika had never met them.

She'd also lost touch with the friends she'd once had.

But she was determined to return one day, face the memories, and maybe learn to love her favorite places again.

When she reached the park near the water, the sight of the trees and open spaces brought her back to the present—this was one of her favorite spots in the city. She took in the birds chirping, the squirrels dashing across trails, and even a few people kicking around a ball on the grass. It reminded her that even if she'd been born in Japan, Vancouver felt more like home to her these days. And she couldn't wait to finally move out of her parents' house and take the city by storm. One day she'd be a big-shot chef, with reservations months in advance; she was sure of it.

Smiling, she strode down one of her usual trails, passing through the mixed trees and abundance of wild, green underbrush that signaled summer in the Pacific Northwest.

As she trailed her fingers over some ferns, she enjoyed the cool shade. The one thing she absolutely did not miss about Japan was late summer. Vancouver never suffered the same kind of humidity and heat.

She walked until she finally came to a bench overlooking the sea, sat down, and took out a pen and small notebook from her backpack. As people walked and played and chatted in the background, she barely noticed as she sketched out ideas for her dream bakery, then jotted down some new recipes she might offer, and finally penned some random culinary ideas to try at home.

Once the light grew dimmer, she finally noticed the sun setting. If she didn't want to miss the last bus, she needed to leave. However, just as she tried to stand, it felt as if something tugged her back and down. The feeling grew stronger, to the point she dropped her notebook and pen and struggled to breathe. Before she could attempt a scream, the world went dark.

Chapter Two

July 1890
London, England

S tone Riley had learned long ago that good things rarely happened to him.

Apart from the vampire Dark Lord of London, Leopold Yates, taking a chance on him despite his dodgy past, his life had been pretty shite up until that point.

His mother had been a whore. One who had sold him at age nine to a fighting ring master for a few quid, which she then spent on the opium that killed her.

Then a few years after that, he'd been sold again to a couple who had treated him as their special pet. They had controlled his every action, and Stone hadn't been able to so much as piss without permission. He'd been made to wear a fucking collar, too. One that had chafed, to the point he still bore the scar.

Years later, he finally had his chance and killed the sadistic bastard and his equally twisted wife. After that, he'd earned money as a prize fighter in the rookeries. At least until the day he caught the notice of Leopold Yates and had started working for the vampire.

It'd been nearly twenty years since he'd finally climbed out of the stews into something bordering on respectable. He was in charge of all security for the Dark Lord's gaming hell, had Yates's trust, and could afford a house of his own, if he wished.

But he preferred living in the flats for employees next door. They were cheap and allowed him to save up his money just in case something went wrong.

Because every day he worried it would all come crashing down.

Which was why it was fucking stupid for him to even be curious about who the time-wielder had managed to bring to London this time. He, she, or they would be a fated one or ones for someone who worked inside the Fated Wheel gaming hell.

Stone should've told Yesenia—the Dark Lord's wife and fae witch time-wielder—to leave him out of her latest matchmaking attempt, but he hadn't for two reasons. One, the fae witch was still learning how to use her magic and the more people she could possibly find a fated one for, the easier it would be for her to grow stronger, and Stone had wanted to help. And two, deep down, in that small part of him that hadn't died and given up all fucking hope when his mother had sold him, he longed to find his fated female.

Not because he believed he deserved love. No, his mother had made sure to tell him repeatedly he was some patron's accident and should be grateful to merely be alive.

However, his sire had been some unnamed vampire, and given how shifter genes were never dominant over fae witches or vampires—only human ones—his vampire half ruled his biology. That included the fact his heart had stopped beating twelve years ago, and he missed being able to fuck.

Of course it felt bloody good, but more than that, he had control over the act, unlike when he'd been the plaything of the couple he'd belonged to for ten years.

Not wanting to relive any of that shite, Stone shoved it aside—he'd become good at suppressing awful memories—and focused on looking scary and threatening. He was known for never smiling, and he wasn't about to start.

However, once his shift ended, he ran into black-haired, light tanned-skinned John Sakamoto, the man of operations for the gaming hell. John blurted, "A female's arrived from the future. Yesenia thinks it'll be easier to have the vampires visit one by one, to see if she bloods them, while she's still unconscious. It didn't work for me, but you're next, Stone. Go up to Yesenia's parlor."

Since vampires merely had to touch someone to determine if they were a fated one—versus shifters who had to fuck and scent an orgasm—it made sense to start with the vampires.

For a second, Stone hesitated, afraid of more rejection. *Fucking ridiculous.* He'd fought and won against hundreds of the strongest males over the years. He'd survived the stews, living on the street, and the twisted games of the arsehole couple who'd owned him.

So why did meeting a female who probably wouldn't end up being his fated one anyway scare the shite out of him?

John lightly slapped his bicep. "Just get it over with, Stone. The female is wearing trousers and strange clothing that Yesenia says is not quite her time but close to it. And when she finally wakes up, it's going to be bloody confusing for her. If Yesenia can figure out who her fated one is first, it might help ease the female into everything."

Given how two people from the future—Yesenia and her brother, River—had already arrived and stirred up trouble, Stone had an inkling of how the female would react. It'd fucking help that two others from the future were here to explain things to the newest arrival.

But one last thing held him back. "Is she human?"

Because if so, it was going to be bloody difficult for him to not be an arse to her. His former owners had shown him the worst parts of humanity.

Just the scent of a full-blooded human triggered a cold sweat and memories of pain.

John shook his head. "Not fully, at least. She has pointed ears, which means she's partially a fae witch."

He paused, his brown eyes turning serious, and added, "And she looks like she could be from the Far East somewhere, although I don't know exactly where."

John and his sister Charlotte were half-Japanese because of their vampire father and put up with a lot of shite from the humans because of it.

The newly arrived female's looks would be a problem if she ever ventured into the human territory.

Stone was already thinking of security plans for her when John shook his head and sighed. "Just fucking go, Stone. Stop standing around and looking scary. I already know you're a tough bastard, but maybe try to be less severe when you see the female."

At least he hadn't asked him to smile. He grunted. "I'll try, although I can't make any promises." John opened his mouth, but Stone turned and headed up the stairs.

To his surprise, the dark-haired pair of Dark Lord Yates and his bride stood in the hallway. Leo's gaze caught his and he nodded. "Stone. And to answer the question in your eyes, River and Nora kicked us out, something about the fewer strangers around the better."

River was a fae witch doctor and had married Leo's sister Nora; they always worked as a team these days.

Stone grunted and was about to ask why John had told him to come here when Yesenia smiled and said, "You shouldn't have to wait much longer. She looked in good health, from what I could tell. So as soon as River gives the all clear, you'll be the next one to see if she's your fated bride."

"Who is she?" he asked.

Yesenia shrugged one shoulder. "Since she didn't arrive with a purse, or driver's license, or anything, I don't know her name, or even where she came from. Her clothes are definitely modern, although the style of her jeans are a little different from the ones in my time."

Like he often did with either Yesenia or River, Stone ignored the strange words that didn't seem important—like driver's license or jeans—and grunted again.

Yesenia shook her head. "You might actually have to speak to her, Stone, if she's your fated one."

He said nothing.

Yesenia sighed. "I know you're not going to become super chatty overnight." The fae witch bit her bottom lip and then blurted, "But try to be nicer than normal, or at least attempt not to grunt and glare all the time. Unlike with River, I have no idea where I ripped her from. For all I know, she might not want to be here."

Ah, the age-old time travel magic debate—was it right to bring fated ones together without asking? Especially since only those of the time-wielder's bloodline could go back to their own time. Anyone else was stuck forever.

But every employee inside the gaming hell knew that if Yesenia didn't practice her magic, she wouldn't be strong enough to fully utilize her powers. And given how some French vampire enemies had moved into London—who probably wanted revenge on the British for slaughtering their females during the war with

Napoleon—the only way to have peace might be for Yesenia to bring their fated ones to this time.

And even that solution had a fucking small chance of success given how they'd kidnapped and tortured the Dark Lord's nephew months ago, all but declaring war.

Regardless of the Dark Lord's politics and enemies, Stone knew what it was like to be thrust into a strange situation without a choice. The female from the future probably wasn't his, but he'd ensure she was protected, no matter who her fated one ended up being. He could at least do that much.

Having no idea what to say to Yesenia—he'd been forbidden to speak for nearly a decade when owned by the human couple, and so talking wasn't easy for him— Stone nodded toward the door. "When can I go in?"

"Let's try and see." She knocked, and soon Nora's voice said to enter. Yesenia poked her head inside the room and a beat later, she gestured. "They signaled it's okay for you to go in."

Taking a deep breath, he stepped inside the large sitting room. The dark-haired, green-eyed Dr. River Vale was next to the chaise lounge near the window, sitting on a stool and putting something back into his medical bag. Stone knew the fae witch from their training sessions—the other male had been working hard to build up his strength to better defend his wife —which meant he could merely nod at River in greeting.

River waved a pale hand toward the female on the red chaise lounge, her body mostly covered with a blanket, and said, "Go ahead and see if she's yours."

He walked closer and paused a beat when he finally saw her face.

She had black hair that fell a little past her shoulders, light tan skin, and the pointed ears of fae witches. She looked young, so fucking young, and yet was easily the most beautiful female he'd ever seen. Her lips looked soft, so soft, and he felt the urge to kiss her.

But then he remembered who he was, and Stone had a hard time believing her radiant, unmarred skin would want his rough, scarred, and calloused hands to touch hers, let alone allow him to kiss her.

Nora Vale—the Dark Lord's sister and now River's wife—said softly beside him, "No need to look like she's about to slit your throat, Stone. Touch her quickly, and we'll know one way or the other."

Mentally cursing himself for letting his usual hard facade slip, he moved closer to the chaise lounge. He wasn't scared, he just bloody well wasn't.

After cracking his knuckles, he leaned down and kept his fingers a hairsbreadth away from hers. *Stop fucking stalling and get it over with.*

If he had a beating heart, he would've taken a deep breath. Instead, he clenched his jaw and brushed his fingers over the back of her small hand.

Time slowed and for a beat, he thought he'd touched her without responding.

Then a deafening sound clambered in his head, and again, as if a church bell was sounding off in his mind. He immediately slapped his palms over his ears, trying to quell the bloody noise. But that did nothing, and the sound sped up little by little into a fucking loud, steady rhythm.

He stumbled back, trying to get away from the noise, but to no avail. A few seconds later, he sucked in a giant gulp of air, and then another, as if he'd die if he didn't take in as much as possible.

With each inhalation, the sound dulled bit by bit. He had no bloody idea how long it'd been, but as his breathing finally slowed, he muttered, "Fuck."

Touching the female had blooded him.

She was his fated bride.

Which now meant he had to bite her, drink her blood, and come inside her at least once, or he'd slowly go mad until he lost his mind.

"Fuck," he repeated as he opened his eyes and stared at the mysterious female. After a beat, he looked from her hands—perfect and dainty—and then to his —massive with his smallest fingers slightly bent from bad breaks—and he wondered how the fuck she was supposed to be his.

He didn't deserve anyone's love, he knew that. But he also didn't deserve such a lovely, young, and innocent-looking bride.

And if she had family she wanted to return to? She was going to hate him forever.

Fuck, fuck, fuck. Why hadn't he asked Yesenia not to include him in her pool of potential candidates? He may have helped his employer's wife, but in the process, he'd bloody well ruined this poor female's life.

Nora was at his side again. "It'll work out, I know it will. I've known you nearly as long as Leo has, and occasionally, I've even seen beyond the wall you've constructed around your true self and heart. Which is why I know you have a protective, caring heart, Stone." She lightly touched his arm. "Don't give up before you've even tried. I nearly did that, and if I had? Then I never would've found the happiness I have now."

If he were the type to speak his mind, he'd point out that Nora was the one with a soft heart, not him.

Stone didn't really acknowledge feelings, apart from those that kept him alive, such as fear or anger.

And yet, as the female shifted a little in her sleep and then settled, the urge to hold her close, growl at anyone who tried to hurt her with words or actions, and never let her out of his sight coursed through him.

His bloody shifter mother had passed on that extra amount of protectiveness. Not that his mother had felt a fucking soft, caring thing toward him. But in general, shifters were even more protective of their fated ones than vampires, and that was saying a lot.

River moved to stand in front of him, his dark brows raised. "I agree, don't look like you're preparing for a fucking funeral, Stone. Besides, on a positive note, you can get hard again. That's something to look forward to, right?" Stone scowled, and River rolled his eyes. "A sense of humor wouldn't kill you. At any rate, I need to make sure the female wakes up and is in good health before Yesenia and I tell her what's going on and you can talk to her. She's most definitely going to need her fucking strength to deal with everything that's about to come crashing down on her."

Stone's gaze moved back to the sleeping female with pointed ears. Crashing down sounded about right.

She might have made his heart beat again, but she was about to wake up to the nightmare of him.

Right then and there, he vowed to do whatever it took to make her life comfortable. Even if she wanted to live apart, to never see him after he claimed her, he'd agree to it.

Because protecting people was what Stone did, and he bloody well would make sure his fated bride was at the top of his list, no matter how she felt about him.

Chapter Three

As Reika slowly woke up, her head pounded, her mouth felt like a desert, and everything ached as if she'd been hit by a bus.

Opening her eyes was hard enough, but even when she managed it, she was in a dark room lit by a handful of candles.

Maybe the power had gone out. Although even in the dim light, she could tell the room wasn't anything in her parents' house. Had some stranger helped her?

Or worse?

A sense of panic crept over her as she struggled to sit up. Her mom had always told her to be careful, that women were snatched off the street every day, and how she didn't like Reika coming home alone after dark.

She'd always brushed off the warnings and hoped her mom hadn't been right.

Don't think of that now. No, Reika would figure out

where she was, what had happened to her, and go from there.

Because even when waking up in a dark, unfamiliar place she was going to remain positive. She had to. Freaking out wouldn't help her.

Slowly she sat up in the large bed, ignoring the little aches in her body she couldn't quite pinpoint. The candles weren't very bright, but she could still make out a fireplace, some cushy chairs, and solid wooden furniture—the bed, a chest of drawers, and even a small desk and chair.

The wooden details and material wallpaper said it was somewhere fancy.

Refusing to believe this was some sort of human trafficking mansion prison—okay, yes, sometimes she was a bit overdramatic in her imagination—she did her best to toss back the blankets and scoot to the edge of the bed, grateful that she still had her clothes on.

Tucking her hair behind her ear, Reika tried to stand up. Immediately her legs gave out and she fell back onto her ass, crying out as a dull pain shot through her body.

Not wanting to let her frustration take over, she checked her arms and hands, but didn't see any bruises or scratches. That ruled out being hit by a car.

Had she been drugged? Although her mind wasn't foggy, or felt thick, or anything like that. Weird.

Just as she tried to stand up again, the door opened, and a single light came on overhead.

Reika barely had time to note it was an old-fashioned bulb when a female and male—both with pointed ears like her—walked in.

But the ears were the only real similarity. The female wore a weird white shirt with huge sleeves and a long, dark blue skirt that someone would wear to a fancy dress party. And the guy wore a black three-piece suit, but a way more formal one than she'd seen on all the people rushing to and from work in downtown Vancouver.

The strange fancy clothes made her think maybe this was a cult, or even a creepy trafficking cult.

The female spoke first, in English. "Hello, my name's Yesenia, and this is my brother, River."

Reika barely had time to note the female had light brown skin and the male was fair, although they both had dark hair, before Yesenia spoke again. "You're probably wondering where the hell you are, right?" On reflex, Reika nodded, and the other female continued, "Well, that's a long story, and complicated to boot. So before we get into that, my brother here is a doctor and would like to examine you. So if you're injured or in pain, let him know."

The male—River, if she remembered right—held up an old-fashioned, leather medical bag, like Reika had seen in TV shows. He also spoke in English. "Yep, just a fae witch doctor wanting to help you. Do you hurt anywhere?"

Both of their accents were different from Vancouver, probably American, although she couldn't place it.

Taking a deep breath, she gathered her courage.

Them being nice to her could be a prelude to something awful, and she wanted to find out what the hell was going on. "Please tell me who you are." She hugged her arms to herself, not wanting to blurt out something about being used for spare parts to sell on the black market. "And where am I?"

Yesenia took a step closer. "You're probably not going to believe me at first."

Her heart rate kicked up, but she did her best not to show it. "Tell me anyway."

River smiled. "You're pretty fucking brave. Awesome. That'll help you in the long run."

Reika frowned but Yesenia's spoke before she did. "Ignore my brother. First tell me if you're hurt. After that, I'll try my best to answer your questions."

Maybe she was naïve, or too trusting, but if they were going to kill her, they would've done so already. No sense in being difficult for no reason, especially if it got her answers. "I have a few aches, and I'm dying of thirst, but otherwise I'm fine."

Yesenia glanced to River, and he nodded. "I'll get you some water and maybe something to eat."

The male left, and Reika let out a sigh. Why, she didn't know. The female could be a murderer or some sort of criminal for all she knew, and be a million times worse than the doctor.

The only good thing was even if Reika wasn't exactly a street fighter and didn't know if she could overpower the other female, at least the odds were even now.

She nearly laughed at the absurdity. Just what had

her life become, thinking about taking down someone in a fight? Some sort of over-the-top TV drama or romance book?

Yesenia pulled out the chair at the desk and sat down, facing her. "There's no how-to guide for this kind of thing, so I'm just going to tell it to you straight. I'm a fae witch who can wield time. My brother and I are originally from the United States in 2022, but this is 1890 London. I was trying to bring a fated one here for someone I know, and that fated one is you." She threw up her hands and said drolly, "Surprise."

Reika blinked. "What are you talking about?"

Yesenia touched her chest. "I'm a time-wielder and brought you here, to 1890, from the future. My guess is probably the 21st century, or even late 20th, since your jeans are a different style than I'm used to seeing. When are you from? Tell me that and I can better fill in the details."

Her heart thundered so hard Reika could barely hear anything else. There was no way she could believe this fae witch. "There are no such things as time-wielders in real life. They only exist in myths and legends."

Yesenia shook her head. "While rare, they are real. I found out by mistake—not even an assessor could pinpoint my powers—and I randomly ended up here, in 1890, by my own power." She gestured at her clothes. "Believe me, I would not be wearing this if given the choice. But wearing pants in this time would be like if I walked around in my underwear out in public back home, not to mention my husband would start killing people for looking at my ass."

Reika barely noticed Yesenia roll her eyes. No, she studied the clothing, the furniture, the single bulb that was clear glass rather than frosted.

Could it be true?

No. There were plenty of hotels and places that catered to certain themes or time periods.

Hell, even if this place were a sex club, she'd take that over being stuck nearly a hundred years before she was even born.

Yesenia's soft voice garnered her attention. "I know this is a lot to take in, and it seems like a dream. But what I say is the truth. The sun should come up soon and if you look out that window, you'll see the horses and carriages, the clothing, the lack of cars and other modern stuff, and you might start to believe me."

Reika shook her head. "No, it's probably just part of a set. There are no time-wielders. Time travel isn't possible."

Yesenia stood, walked toward the bed, and looked her dead in the eye. "It *is* possible, I promise you. If I need to get my vampire husband or my vampire sister-in-law to tell you that—which you know as well as I do that they can't lie—I will. They'll both say the same as me."

As she stared at Yesenia's face, Reika's heart pounded harder.

She was right—vampires couldn't lie. And if two were willing to come in and tell her the same thing, it meant it must be true.

Somehow, some way, time travel magic existed.

No. She couldn't be in the past. Surely there were rules about taking people without asking.

Weren't there?

Damn, she really should've studied the Code of Fae Witches more during her magical training years.

Yesenia spoke again, her tone softer. "I know it's a lot to take in. I do. But for now, let's just start at the beginning, as if we'd met on the street. What's your name? Where are you from? Knowing that might help me speed some things along and get you adjusted faster." She paused and then murmured, "Because you can't go back to whenever you're from."

What? She leaned forward. "I can't go back to 2003? To Vancouver? Why?"

Yesenia smiled sympathetically. "No, I'm afraid you're stuck here. Time travel is one way for anyone outside of my bloodline."

A sense of panic started to creep over her. "Say this is all true for a second, why would you do that to me? Snatch me from my home, my family, my everything?"

The other female raised a hand as if to touch her, and then dropped it. "I'm sorry. I truly am. There's some debate about finding fated ones and moving them through time without asking, although the fae witch council usually allows it. But the main reason you're here is far more serious—there are a lot of people relying on me to strengthen my magical muscles to help bring about peace. Despite my age, I only found out I had magic earlier this year. There's more to it, of course, but I can't share any more just yet."

She stared at the determination and fierceness in Yesenia's gaze; she believed her own words, most likely.

Reika didn't want to believe the female, she really didn't. Time travel magic was something that existed only in the myths. No one in living memory had ever met one, and that had seemed like enough proof.

And yet, what if it were true? Some magical abilities were rarer than others, although they usually never went dormant for hundreds of years, or whatever.

Reika glanced up at the old-fashioned lightbulb with the bright filament and then away, the shape still highlighted in her vision for a few seconds.

Time-wielders were only in the stories.

Weren't they?

And yet, as she looked around the room again, there were no electrical outlets, no TV, not even an alarm clock or a radio. Just the one lightbulb overhead.

Add in the strange clothing and the doctor's medical bag, and Reika wondered if maybe she'd died after all and woken up in some strange in-between place. That would make more sense than ending up in the past.

Yesenia took her hand and squeezed. The action brought her back to the moment. "Listen, I know this is a lot to take in, and once it's light outside, maybe glancing out the window and seeing Victorian London will make it all the more real. But for now, can you just tell me your name?"

Wanting any sort of distraction, she whispered, "Reika."

"Ray-kah. I don't think I've heard that one before, but it's such a pretty name."

People always mentioned it was new to them, and so Reika seized on something normal and expected to keep her from thinking she was either crazy or dead. "It means beautiful flower."

Yesenia nodded. "Better than mine." She scrunched her nose. "Yesenia means palm tree."

The other female snorted and despite everything, Reika nearly smiled. Then she glanced back at the strange light bulb and blurted, "Is this really the past?"

"Yeah, I'm afraid so. It's totally my fault you're here, by the way. So if you're going to hate anyone, let it be me and no one else."

She met Yesenia's brown-eyed gaze again. "If it's true—and I still don't quite believe it—why me? You mentioned a fated one, but fae witches don't have them."

Or half fae witch in her case, but that didn't change the fact.

"Ah, but that's where things get complicated. My brother and I are fae witches, but this is the vampire's territory in London." She paused and added, "You're the fated bride of a half vampire and half shifter named Stone Riley. But you won't have to meet him until you're ready, of course. Although you couldn't ask for a better person to look out for you in a new place. He's like a secret service agent to the max, but a sort of movie star one. He's silent but sexy."

Reika had barely frowned at that comment when River returned with a tray. After a glance at her, he raised an eyebrow. "Dropped the truth early, didn't you, Senia?"

As Yesenia stuck out her tongue at her brother, Reika thought maybe they wouldn't be murdering her, or selling her, or carving her up for body parts after all.

Maybe.

Focus, Reika. Right, she needed to hear what this fae witch had to say about her supposed fated guy, or whatever. "How does this Stone Riley dude know I'm his?"

Yesenia shrugged. "Simple, really—he touched your skin while you were unconscious, and you blooded him. I know, I know, maybe not the best way to go about it, letting random people touch you while passed out. But I'm still new at this and will try to do better in the future."

Great. A new time-wielder who didn't really know what she was doing.

Wait, was she now accepting Yesenia had time travel magic?

Rubbing her face with her hands, she tried to gather her thoughts.

Yes, she was half shifter, but her fae witch half was dominant. It meant she didn't have a fated one.

Although if the guy was also half shifter like her, did that change anything? Did those two halves seek out a fated one?

If only she could remember the finer details of her paranormal studies from her school days.

Although if this Stone guy was also part vampire,

then she knew his vampire half would be dominant, meaning he definitely had a fated one.

Her.

Or so Yesenia had said.

Maybe if she were back home and discovered something like this, she could be more positive about it. She'd always secretly hoped for a fated one like the vampires or shifters. After all, her mom had been her dad's and they'd had a great love story. If not for his death, they'd still be together.

But then it hit her—if she was really in the past, then as far as the myths said, she couldn't go back.

She'd never see her mom or stepdad ever again.

Unless they ended up here too.

Sadness rushed forth, but she pushed it back. She refused to cry in front of these strangers. No, instead she focused on the million and one questions racing through her head. She needed answers. "Can you bring anyone here, to this time, from the future?"

As Yesenia bit her lip, Reina's heart squeezed. The fae witch's words only confirmed her suspicions. "Eventually. Right now, I'm sort of in training. I know, I know, I'm nearly twenty-nine now but I only found out I had magic earlier this year. And there are so many rules about who can or can't come." She took Reika's hand. "But I promise, once I'm fully trained, and if the fae witch Dark Lord doesn't have any objections, I can bring your family here. Well, if you think they'd want to come."

A flicker of hope flashed in her chest. Although asking her parents to give up everything to reside in the past seemed like too much. She whispered, "I-I don't know."

Yesenia hunched down until she was eye level with Reika. "You aren't married with children, are you?"

She shook her head. "No. But I'm all my mom has, apart from my stepdad."

Silence fell for a few beats until River finally spoke up. "All of this is a hell of a lot for anyone to take in. Allow me to give you a quick check with my magic, heal what needs repairing, and then we'll leave you to eat and let it all set in. You won't have to meet Stone until you're ready."

Is solitude what she wanted?

While she still wavered on the whole being-in-the-past thing, Reika liked to make plans. To know what she was going to do, or how to overcome a problem. Just like when she'd first moved to Canada and could barely ask in English for someone's name, she wasn't about to allow anything to bring her down or hold her back.

Okay, Reika. Focus on what you can do instead of what you can't.

Determination and hope were her two best coping mechanisms. Maybe soon she'd wake up and find out this was all a dream anyway.

Or maybe not.

In case of the latter, she needed to believe Yesenia could bring her parents here.

Because she didn't want to think of how it'd destroy her mom to lose her without a word.

However, even if the time-wielder could reunite

her, life would still be a challenge. There were a million reasons it might not be so rosy—she was a Japanese female in 1890 London, or so they said—and it'd be difficult. Racism would be a lot worse, not to mention misogyny would be off the charts. But she hadn't worked so hard for so many years, first with learning English and starting over in Canada, and later perfecting her culinary skills and blending it with her magic, to give up now.

She needed to find a way to make it work. She just had to.

The words helped, although her heart squeezed at the thought of never seeing her home again, never walking through the park, or debuting a new treat at the bakery.

Never hugging her mom, or even rolling her eyes at her stepdad's corny jokes.

Never visiting her hometown in Japan again.

Suddenly, putting everything off until later seemed like a huge mistake.

Stop it, Reika. This isn't you. Find the positive and move forward. Keep busy and find a way.

Taking a deep breath, she did her best to calm her heart and push away her doubts. Until she knew everything, she shouldn't worry. Much. She'd just put one foot in front of the other and keep moving forward.

Both Yesenia and River stared at her, waiting to see what she'd say. Since she wasn't about to sob, or scream, or throw a tantrum, she cleared her throat and decided to be practical. She could use a distraction, after all. "Can I get some paper and a pen? I want to write a few things down."

River shrugged. "I'll see what I can find. Although a pencil might be easier as ballpoint pens are few and far between in this time, and writing with a pen nib and ink is fucking difficult."

Reika shrugged. "Either will work. I had to do brush and ink calligraphy in elementary school, so I'm sure a pen whatever is easier to use."

Although why she was blabbering about her childhood *shodo* classes, she had no idea.

River and Yesenia shared a glance before the female asked, "And will you at least think about meeting Stone, the guy you blooded? I'm not saying you have to let him claim you right away or anything, but he's been stalking around the place, growling about needing to ensure your safety, and maybe meeting you will calm him down a little. Er, wait, that makes him sound unhinged. He's not really, though. Did I mention he's sexy in a silent, growly way?"

River rolled his eyes. "Make him sound creepier, why don't you?" He looked at Reika. "He's a good guy to have at your back, although don't tell him I said that."

Yesenia added, "And you wouldn't meet with him alone. One or both of us would be there too. And since Stone's basically a vampire despite his mixed heritage, he can't lie without some discomfort, even if it's not as extreme as a full-blooded vamp. So there's that."

Even though it could end up being really stupid, she

had to admit she was curious about this silent, sexy Stone guy.

Before she could talk some sense into her head about waiting until she knew she was safe and not being fed a lot of crap about being in the past, her stomach rumbled. Loudly. She eyed the tray River had brought in, but all she saw were slightly burnt bread rolls, a teapot, and some jam in a little bowl.

If she *were* a prisoner, that would be the kind of junk they'd give her.

However, she now had an idea of how to test her boundaries. Besides, being in a kitchen would calm her down more than anything. "I'll meet him if I can bake some real bread or food in the kitchen at the same time." She paused, but her magic wasn't going to be a secret for long, so she added, "My magic lets me improve the taste of anything organic, even better if I make it myself. And that bread just looks really sad. Do you actually eat that charcoal?"

River grimaced. "The cook is new, and not the best, I'll admit. I may not live here anymore—thank fuck—but I visit with my wife often enough that I know how shitty the food is."

Right, a purpose. "Then let me whip something up."

Yesenia smiled. "Sounds like a plan. And if you need to use the bathroom, we can swing by one of the flushing toilets. They aren't in every room, and I know it's one of the things I would miss the most from the future, if I didn't have it."

Reika hadn't even thought of that. Toilets were just

there, because just about everyone had one. At least in Canada.

Each new revelation only cemented she was in the past. But she wasn't going to accept it just yet.

She tested out her legs and managed to stay upright. "Yeah, the toilet sounds good and then straight to the kitchen." She gestured toward the really sad-looking roll. "Don't let any paranormal or human eat that thing either."

River snorted, but Yesenia ignored him. She moved to the door and opened it. "Come on, then. The kitchen for the family is the same one used for the gaming hell, and it's in the sort of basement area of the building."

She frowned. "Gaming what?"

"Gaming hell. It's what they call casinos here. With time, you'll probably end up with a list of all the words and phrases they use in 1890 versus back home. I nearly have a notebook full by this point."

And as Yesenia rambled about terms, and language, and nothing of importance, her voice soothed Reika a little. But it wasn't until she stepped inside the giant kitchen that two things happened.

One, the sights, sounds, and smells of cooking fed her soul.

And two, judging by the oven and other things in the kitchen, it wasn't up to 2003 standards.

River stated, "I'll get Stone while you get started. The sooner he stops glaring at everyone, the better."

Reika barely noted the male leave. No, she couldn't stop staring at the oven.

It was some sort of metal—cast iron?—thing, long, with several metal doors that swung to the side on the bottom half. A grate in the middle showed the bright orange and red heat of coal. The surface had a few pots on it, with at least one boiling.

No sign of a gas or electric oven. No refrigerator, either, let alone a dishwasher. Just lots of tables, a really big sink with running water, copper pans hanging on the walls, and lots of shelves full of dishes and jars. A few lights overhead were the only electrical-type thing in sight.

It was like a kitchen from some period drama or something.

Yesenia squeezed her shoulder. "Welcome to 1890, where cast iron coal stoves are the thing and everything, I mean everything, is washed by hand."

Even if this was the past—it looked more and more like it was—Reika wouldn't let something like a weird coal stove stop her.

No, cooking and using her magic would give her strength, settle her nerves, and give her something edible to eat. A full belly always helped make things better.

Standing tall, she gestured toward the stove. "Then someone had better show me how to use it."

And soon enough she was looking through the pantry, finding the necessary dishes, and doing everything she could to focus on cooking instead of everything that was missing from a modern-day kitchen.

Chapter Four

Stone strode toward the kitchen, uncaring if River kept up with him or not.

His fated bride was awake and willing to see him.

He held no fucking illusions about her instantly smiling at him and falling into his arms. But his instinct wanted to at least talk with her and ensure she was safe.

He couldn't offer her much, but protection was one thing he could.

River growled, "Wait, Stone. I haven't finished telling you what not to do."

He grunted and ignored the fae witch. Even if his main job was security at the Fated Wheel, Stone sometimes helped Ambrose Yates—the Dark Lord's nephew—with the rescue of abused or enslaved paranormals. Just because Stone was muscled, and tall, and could make lesser males cower with a look didn't mean he couldn't be gentle or less intimidating when necessary.

Reaching the door to the kitchens, he stopped and turned toward River. "I won't hurt her."

River frowned. "Of course not. But she's just been ripped from everything she knows and is pretty damn vulnerable."

He nodded in reply before walking into the kitchen.

It took less than a second to find her. She was frowning down at the range, watching as a kitchen maid explained how to stoke the coals and adjust the heat.

Awake, the female looked less young. Her unbound hair stopped just past her shoulders, and while it was unusual to see a female without her hair pulled up, it seemed to suit her.

As his gaze traveled her body, he resisted growling. He didn't like how she wore trousers, which displayed her shapely arse and legs to the world.

Taking off his jacket, he strode over and placed it on her shoulders. Since he was so much taller, it at least covered her arse, if not all of her legs.

Her eyes met his—a deep brown that was almost black—and his instinct clamored to toss her over his shoulder and cart her away.

Then he'd tease her slowly and make her beg for his cock, until he could bite her neck and thrust inside her.

Yesenia spoke and broke through his fantasy. "Stone, it's like a million degrees in front of the stove. She doesn't need your jacket. Take it back."

He grunted but kept his gaze on his fated female. "Trousers are indecent."

She blinked up at him. "What are you talking about?"

Her accent was similar to the Vale siblings, although a little different. A far cry from London, that was for sure. "Females shouldn't wear trousers. It may give males ideas."

She raised a black eyebrow. "No, males just need to restrain themselves and keep it in their pants. That's not my job."

Yesenia tried to interrupt. "Stone—"

But he kept going, talking more than he had for months, if not years. "No matter what they should do, the reality is they'll still act. Walk around like that outside, and you'll draw every predatory male or female right to you. Wear a skirt. It's safer."

She pushed off the jacket and pressed it to his chest. He should be mad at her actions, but even through the layers of fabric between them, her touch heated his skin in a way no female had before.

His cock definitely took notice and the image of her hands pinned over her head as he claimed her flashed into his mind.

Get some bloody control. As he pushed aside the images, he scowled at the female. If she'd been similarly affected, he couldn't tell. Her cheeks were already flushed from tending to the range, and her heart had already been racing when he'd entered. There were also too many scents in the kitchen to tell if she were aroused or not.

His instinct didn't like that one fucking bit.

When she replied, her tone was brisk. "Right now,

I'm hungry, and tired, and cranky. Once I eat something, then we can talk about your caveman tendencies. But for now? Get out of the way so I can cook some food."

She turned away from him, and he replied, "It's my job to protect you. I'm Stone Riley, and you're my fated bride."

The female didn't turn around and merely waved a hand in dismissal. "Food first and then I'll deal with you."

His jaw dropped a little and then he remembered others were watching, and he promptly closed it. "Fine, but I'm not letting you out of my sight until you change into some proper clothes."

That came out a bit huskier than he intended, probably because he couldn't stop staring at her arse. He wondered how her softness would feel against his hardness, and if she would like to feel his hand caress and slap her bum. Would she let him take her from behind?

Fuck. What was wrong with him? Stone didn't have constant sex fantasies. If he had a need, he sated it, end of story. But it had never been something to dream about, let alone crave with everything he had. Nor had he ever suffered an aching, hard cock that didn't seem to soften, no matter how many people were in the room.

It had to be some fated bride instinct magic. Or possibly his shifter side trying to push him toward fucking her to revel in the scent of her orgasm. His vampire side may be dominant, but the shifter side had needs too.

He barely resisted running a hand over his face. *Bloody hell.* He needed her to change clothes, and sooner rather than later, or he'd never be able to think clearly.

He growled for good measure, but his fated bride continued her tasks and ignored him.

Because of course she wouldn't be intimidated by him. That would be too easy, and Stone's life had never been fucking easy.

Yesenia chuckled, and he glared at her. She gestured toward the prickly fae witch. "Say hello to Reika, Stone. I think you've finally met your match."

REIKA'S HEART POUNDED, grateful the heat of the range kept everyone from seeing her blush.

True, the fire from the coals was super hot, and having a tall, broad-shouldered male standing less than a foot away, radiating his own inferno, didn't help.

But the blush was from touching him and having him stare down at her with his intense, almost golden gaze. His brown hair and chiseled jaw all but screamed masculine, as did his broad chest. A solid, muscled chest, judging from when she'd thrust the coat back at him.

And instead of being super pale like most vampires, he was tanned, as if he spent time in the sun.

Most vampires couldn't handle that much sunshine, but half vampires could.

If she were back home and had met the tanned, sexy, growly male, she probably would've been a little nicer to him. Who knows, she might've tried flirting, even though she was super bad at it.

But a hungry Reika was a cranky one, and she didn't have the energy to be charming or flirtatious. Besides, if she were his fated one, he'd want to claim her regardless.

Especially since he'd go crazy if she didn't sleep with him and let him drink from her once.

So screw putting on airs—she was going to be herself.

Not wanting to think more about fated ones, or Stone's tall, large body thrusting over her, Reika walked over to the large table in the middle of the room. The kitchen maid had already laid out the ingredients she'd asked for, thank goodness.

And while she'd have bread baking soon enough— the cook had taken one look at Reika, ordered her out of the kitchen, and quit when Yesenia told her no, which meant she would have to teach the remaining kitchen maids later—she'd start with omelets.

As she chopped the vegetables and then whisked the eggs and milk, she did her best not to lift her head and stare at Stone.

But she could feel his gaze. Oh, how she could feel his gaze. It was like some sort of heated laser beam aimed straight at her.

Was it always this way between fated ones? Or was it just because the male didn't say much and had the most intense eyes she'd ever seen?

She took everything to the stove and glanced quickly to the side of the room. Stone had his arms crossed over his chest, a hard expression on his face.

For a split second, she wondered if he ever smiled, let alone laughed.

While she should probably just ignore him, most of the kitchen staff had left with the cook and she needed all the help she could get. So she gestured toward the table and said, "The ingredients and recipe for the bread is over there. Can you mix it all up for me while I cook this?"

He blinked. "What?"

She smiled. "Don't you want to be useful?"

"I—" He started and then stopped.

Yesenia laughed from her stool at the long table but didn't interject.

Reika ignored her and stated, "You can either help or get out of my kitchen. I need to concentrate and you staring at me isn't helping."

He frowned and for a beat, Reika wondered if she'd have to ask someone to physically get him out. Then he grumbled something unintelligible and went to the bowl and ingredients. He lifted a measuring cup, held it high, dipped it into the flour, and made a show of dumping it into the bowl.

He waited, as if he wanted praise for the simple task. Men weren't so different here in that respect— they wanted recognition for doing something minimal. "Good job. Now do the rest. Otherwise, I won't share my omelets with you."

She turned before he could speak, but she heard a low growl.

He really was a growly one.

Although she secretly loved each and every one as they rolled over her and made parts of her ache and tingle. Parts she shouldn't be thinking with as she handled the giant cast iron stove.

No sex dreams in the kitchen. Sticking to her new rule, she started frying vegetables in the pan with grease. It wasn't long before Stone grunted, and she nearly shivered at the deep sound. She resisted looking at him but wondered what was wrong with her. Here she was, who the hell knew where, in a strange place, and maybe even in the past. She shouldn't like or lust after any male, no matter how sexy.

She focused on the coal stove and not burning or undercooking her food. Somehow she managed to cook three edible omelets, and once they were done, she turned, only to find Stone standing a foot away from her.

She hadn't even heard him move.

His golden eyes glared down. The focused gaze made her heart race.

Somehow, she kept her voice even as she said, "Excuse me, I need to get through."

He held up his bowl, pressed it into her free arm, and then turned and went back to his post on the far side of the room. As he crossed his arms over his chest, she blurted, "You really don't talk a lot, do you?"

He grunted and said nothing.

But for a split second, his lips twitched. That was probably his equivalent of a full-blown grin.

She smiled at him on purpose and his brows drew together.

Shrugging, she put the bowl down—the bread needed to rise—and took the three plates with omelets, placing one in front of Yesenia, another at her spot, and the third across the table from her seat. She gestured. "That's for you, Stone, if you can spare a few minutes from glare duty."

Yesenia snorted, but Reika was too hungry to reply. She dug into her first bite and moaned. Even if the stove was a bit iffy, her magic had helped to make it taste delicious.

Stone halted behind his stool and stared at her. She swallowed. "What?"

Shaking his head, he sat down. And despite wanting to inhale her food, she watched Stone take his first bite. He didn't moan, but his eyes widened.

"Good, huh?"

He nodded and tucked in.

Yeah, he definitely wasn't a talker.

And yet, she didn't seem to mind.

Chapter Five

S tone had never eaten anything as good as what the
chit had made him. River had explained about
Reika's magic, and if his now-empty plate was any sign,
she was extremely skilled with it.

And if he were truly trying to win her, or thought
she'd want him for more than a quick tumble, he'd tell
her so.

But he had too many issues, too much in his past,
and he wouldn't risk the floodgates opening by
encouraging Reika.

So he remained silent and waited for her to finish.
She took dainty bites, moaning without realizing it, and
it took everything he had not to adjust his hard cock.

Thankfully Yesenia spoke up, which stopped Reika's
little delicious noises. "You really can cook, Reika. The
only other time I remember things being this good was
when my stepmother was alive. She had the ability to
make things grow to their very best—the biggest, the

tastiest, the easiest to grow, you name it. I don't remember her being an amazing cook, but if the ingredients were like crack, she couldn't really mess it up."

Stone watched Yesenia a beat. He didn't know much about her past, really. Or, rather, the future to him, which was still her past.

Bloody time-travel magic made things confusing as fuck.

Reika laid down her cutlery. "My plan had been to hire a fae witch like that, once I finally was able to open my own restaurant." She glanced down at the table and played with her plate. "Although I suppose that doesn't really matter any longer."

The previously brave, headstrong female had disappeared.

And Stone didn't like it.

He grunted. "Why? People eat here too."

Stone ignored Yesenia's startled look and focused entirely on Reika. She finally raised her eyes and met his gaze.

He bloody hated the flash of sadness and uncertainty there. He wanted to haul her into his lap and promise Reika the world.

Pushing his ridiculous thought aside, Stone focused on her answer. "Well, yeah, of course. But I have nothing—no family, no savings, not even a job or a place to live. How am I supposed to open a restaurant?"

Yesenia opened her mouth, but Stone beat her to it. "You could start here. Get Leo's kitchen in order until he finds a new cook, and I'm sure the Dark Lord will pay you well. In the meantime, I can look for a place that would make a good restaurant space for you."

As soon as the words left his mouth, Stone wondered what the hell he was doing. She wasn't his to keep, never would be, so why was he offering her a future?

He must be acting on his combined vampire and shifter instincts.

Then Reika surprised him by raising an eyebrow and stating, "You're trying to bribe me so I'll let you claim me, right?"

He frowned. That hadn't been his first thought, no.

But to say that aloud might give her the wrong idea. He wasn't trying to woo her.

Was he?

Yesenia cleared her throat. "Before we start planning a grand opening, there are a few things Reika needs to do first." She pushed her plate out of the way and leaned on the table. "You're obviously a fae witch, but is that all?"

Reika shook her head. "My mother is a fae witch, but my father was an Asian bear shifter."

The female was half shifter as well? Well, fuck, that would explain some of his pull toward her then. Shifter halves weren't dominant, but they bloody well played a role in protecting and claiming a fated one, mixed heritage and all.

Yesenia smiled and waved toward him. "Half shifter, just like Stone. That should make the claiming superhot and sexy." He narrowed his eyes at Yesenia and grunted, but the fae witch shrugged. "What? I thought even in this time, male paranormals didn't get all bashful and shy about sex."

Crossing his arms over his chest, he glared at her for a beat. "We have a guest."

Reika cleared her throat and waved a hand in the air. "Hello, I'm sitting right here. And it's fine, I've heard worse from some of my coworkers. That's what happens when you work with a lot of university students." Since he remained silent—just the thought of her talking about sex with strangers stirred his instinct to cart her away—Reika asked, "What's your shifter half?"

Not that it really mattered since half-shifters couldn't change forms. "Wolf."

She nodded. "That suits you. Because I don't know if anyone's ever told you, but you're super growly."

Yesenia laughed, but Stone merely shook his head. She was amusing, but it wasn't as if he wanted to get close to her.

After standing, he retreated a few steps from the table. "I need to go to work soon, so I'll find you tomorrow."

He turned to leave, but Reika saying, "Stone," made him halt and look over his shoulder.

After he raised an eyebrow in question, she said, "Thanks for helping in the kitchen. I might need to put you to work again later."

He shrugged and left the room.

But as much he tried to focus on the upcoming night's security, and staff rotations, and the myriad

other details related to his job, his head filled with
images of him working next to Reika as the heat of the
stove made her flush. A bead of sweat would trail down
her face, and he'd lick it, nibble at her jaw, and lift her
onto the table before tossing up her skirts—she'd be
wearing skirts in his fantasy—and devour what he
really wanted to taste—her sweet cunny.

The images kept replaying to the point he had to
dump a pitcher of cold water over his head before
changing into his work attire.

Staying away from his fated bride was going to be
bloody difficult, but he'd survived worse.

REIKA HAD WANTED Stone to stay a little while longer,
but she knew he had a job and a life of his own. Her
just appearing out of nowhere didn't mean he'd drop
everything to spend time with her.

After all, this wasn't some sort of rom-com movie
or anything. No, it was more like some weird B-movie
where a girl from the future ends up as a cook for a
bunch of vampires.

Not that she minded the work, even with the
strange equipment and newly hired staff—although
where Leo had found them on such short notice, she
had no idea.

After Leo had tasted her cooking and hired her
temporarily, Reika got the staff fed without burning
herself or the food. And by the time she had to cook
orders for the casino customers, she'd become rather

skilled. The busy hours had made her feel useful and almost helped her forget that she was stuck in the past.

At least she had a guaranteed place to stay—a guest room inside the casino everyone else here called a gaming hell. Oh, and she had complete control over what to serve, with a few suggestions.

Too bad finding ingredients for any of her Japanese-inspired dishes would be difficult in 1890 London.

And yes, she'd accepted she was in the past. After changing into a button-up blouse—no giant sleeves, thank goodness, to catch fire in the kitchen—and a long skirt, Yesenia had taken Reika outside and walked her down the street. Seeing carriages, old-fashioned shops with weird hats and dresses, and the complete lack of any sort of modern technology had sealed it.

What she hadn't been able to fully confront was the fact she was stuck here and might never see her family again.

No, she'd shoved that stuff deep down, to deal with later. Instead, she'd used her magic and cooked, creating the happy place that could calm her down from anything.

Things whirled by so quickly that she barely noticed when the orders stopped coming, or how she was probably pretty gross from sweating in front of the stove, or how her apron hadn't caught everything and her clothes needed washing.

When a maid finally announced the patron orders were closed for the day, Reika let out a sigh and dabbed her brow with a wet cloth. The basement kitchen was so much hotter than anything she'd used before, that was for sure. No doubt due to the lack of ventilation.

Needing more than an already warm cloth to cool down, she went to the biggest window facing the alley and opened it. Even if the air wasn't exactly fresh and invigorating—there was far too much coal smoke and horse dung—the light breeze made her sigh and lean into it.

Reika didn't know how long she stood there before she was suddenly yanked back as the window slammed shut. She was then whirled around to face Stone, his eyes blazing with anger. "What the bloody hell were you doing?"

He'd hauled her up against him, and for a second, she had a hard time focusing on anything but his tall, muscled body pressed against hers.

Her inner shifter wanted to tear his clothes off and lick every inch of his skin.

Not allowing that thought to show on her face, she focused on her anger. "I didn't realize standing at a window was off-limits. If you couldn't tell, it's crazy hot in here."

He hauled her further from the window, down the narrow hall, and into the small room used by the cook and the housekeeper to go over the accounts.

Stone shut the door and growled down at her. "This is a gaming hell. Around closing time, all sorts of bloody criminals and dangerous people lurk about. Pickpockets, debt collectors, and maybe even one of our greatest threats at present—the French vampires. They could've slit your throat or hauled you through the window or pushed you aside and crawled through, holding you down as they forced themselves on you." He shook her a little. "It's fucking dangerous around here at night."

Normally she'd be mad about some male shouting at her. But fear shone in his eyes, mixed in with his anger, and Reika softened a fraction. "Is it really that bad?"

"Inside I can protect you. We all can." He waved toward the wall. "Out there, alone, you don't stand a chance."

For a second, her heart raced and her breathing sped up at the sight of Stone so animated, so afraid for her.

But then she remembered if he couldn't claim her once, he'd go crazy. Keeping her alive was paramount to him staying sane. She wouldn't read into it.

However, when he leaned closer, his hot breath dancing against her face, she couldn't look away from his eyes. Need flashed in them before quickly vanishing.

His gaze dropped to her mouth and heat spread throughout her body, ending between her thighs. Even her nipples stood at attention, and it took everything she had not to rub against his hard chest and moan at the friction.

When his golden-eyed gaze met hers again, she murmured, "Stone."

For a few beats, he froze, his gaze uncertain. Then he growled, pressed her even closer against him, and kissed her.

T<small>HE SIGHT</small> of Reika standing at the open window, her eyes closed and oblivious to danger, had kicked Stone's instincts into gear.

Soon he was holding her close as he scolded her, trying to tame the flash of fear that had torn through him at the thought of someone harming her.

Then, aware of everyone in the kitchen, he'd taken her into the small room used by the cook and housekeeper. It put them even closer together, the space soon filling up with her sweet scent. Despite his best efforts, his gaze had moved to her lips.

After she murmured his name, his control snapped. He needed to taste her, to reassure his instinct she was still here and alive.

So he crushed his lips to hers and hauled her soft body against his, groaning at the feel of her full, warm lips.

She clung to his shirt, tilted her head, and parted her lips. It was all the invitation he needed to lick, and lap, and explore every inch of her mouth. As she met him stroke for stroke, he groaned, relieved she wasn't some shy miss who would scream and slap him.

His hands traveled down her back, to her arse, and he rocked her against his hard cock as he continued to dominate her with his kiss.

She writhed against him, and he nearly nicked her lips with his elongated fangs.

Not wanting her to come until he had his mouth on her cunt, he broke the kiss to trail his lips down her neck, to between her breasts, and back up again, wishing her bloody clothes weren't in the way.

He had his hand on her shirt—about ready to pull and pop off her buttons so he could free her tits and suckle her perfect little nipples—when someone banged on the door behind him.

"Stone, open up!"

He broke the kiss. "Fuck."

It was Leo.

Despite the Dark Lord shouting for him to open the door, he took a second to take in Reika's flushed face, swollen lips, and slightly disheveled hair. Even though he'd never been tender with a female in his life, he couldn't resist brushing the stray strands off her face and tucking them behind her ear.

She searched his gaze. "That was…"

"Stone!"

With a growl, he released Reika, turned, and opened the door. The ruler of all vampires in southern England, Leo Yates, narrowed his brown eyes, peered behind Stone to Reika and back again. "One of the maids was worried you might throttle her."

He glared. "I'd never hurt her."

Leo shrugged. "I know that. However, I wanted to check on Reika." Leo pushed his way into the small room, which put him extremely close to Stone's female. He growled and Leo put up a hand to silence him. "I have my own bride, remember? I have no interest in yours."

He knew that, of course. And yet, Stone's instinct

didn't like another male standing so close to his fae witch. Especially since he hadn't claimed her yet.

Leo turned his attention back to Reika. "Are you all right?"

She cleared her throat, smoothed her hair, and held her head high.

Even when facing one of the most powerful vampires in Europe, Reika didn't back down. It made him want to cheer and praise her.

She replied, "I'm fine. Stone and I were, er, getting to know each other better."

Leo glanced at him and back to Reika. "Well, I'd rather you save that kind of getting to know each other until a few more days have passed. You've just arrived."

Stone growled. "She's not a child, Leo."

"Of course not. But until Khan talks with her and decides her fate, you need to postpone the claiming."

Reika blurted, "Who's Khan?"

Leo replied, "He's the Dark Lord in charge of the fae witches. Since your fae witch side is dominant, he'll have the final say in what you can or cannot do with regards to your magic."

Reika frowned. "I'm not going to have to kiss his ring or something silly like that, am I?"

Leo snorted. "The French and Spaniard Dark Lords have bloody ridiculous practices, but not here in England. However, be precise when asking him for something. Khan doesn't like people who constantly change their minds."

Reika asked, "When will I meet him?"

Leo shrugged. "Tomorrow afternoon. Given how

it's late, you should retire now and try to get some sleep. I can escort you upstairs, if you like."

Stone took a step toward Reika. "I can take her to her room."

Leo raised his brows. "Will you be able to keep your hands off her?"

Reika clapped her hands. "For crying out loud, I'm standing right here. Why does everyone keep talking as if I'm invisible? Just because English wasn't my first language doesn't mean I can't understand you. I lived in Canada longer than Japan, you know."

Stone ignored Leo to look at Reika. "Yesenia wants us to look out for you whilst you adjust. Although compared to the stories I've heard, you're definitely calmer about being brought to the past."

She smiled. "Well, it's a shock, for sure. But I always try to find the best in every situation. And freaking out or crying won't help me."

The image of Reika sobbing into a pillow flashed into his mind, and it made Stone want to hit the wall. No bride of his should ever have to cry.

Fuck. He really needed to stop thinking of her as his long-term. "No matter what happens, you can ask me for anything. I will always help you."

As they stared at one another, something passed between them, and her smile wrapped around Stone's heart.

He'd never known kindness, or playfulness, or any sort of light emotion until he'd started working for Leo.

And even then, the experiences had been few and far between.

However, just being with Reika made everything seem a little bit brighter. As if her smiles, and laughter, and sunny presence could make each and every day the best one yet.

Bloody hell. When had he started to become so romantic?

He needed to stop, though. Because if she ever learned of his past, of the things he'd been forced to do to stay alive, she wouldn't want anything to do with him.

Leo cleared his throat and broke the moment. "I'm not leaving you two alone in here. So let's go to the kitchen and I'll arrange for the maids to clean up whilst we both escort Reika to her room."

Stone glared at Leo. Many wouldn't, but he knew the Dark Lord well, had his complete trust, and was one of a handful allowed to show disrespect in private. "I will take her."

Leo opened his mouth, but Reika spoke first. "I won't go to bed until the kitchen is clean. I never ask others to do what I won't do myself, and I need to earn the trust of the staff here. Both of you can go to bed, and I'll ask one of the night guards to take me to my room."

"No," Stone stated.

Reika raised her brows. "So all the people saying I can trust the staff here, including Leo himself, were lying?"

"Of course not, but—"

"Then I don't see the problem. Unless you're going to stay and help me clean up, I'll see you tomorrow."

He ignored Leo's snort. "I'll help you clean up then."

She smiled at him. "The thought of seeing such a tall, muscled male wearing an apron and washing dishes would be really funny."

He frowned. "I never said I'd wear an apron."

"But maybe you should. That way you'll be less intimidating to the kitchen maids."

He grunted. "It's my job to be intimidating."

She shrugged. "Apron required, Mr. Riley."

Laughter danced in Reika's eyes. She probably expected him to say no and storm off.

But he was a stubborn bastard, and he wanted to escort her to her room. So he replied, "Well, then give me an apron and a task, and I'll do it."

Leo chuckled, opened the door leading out of the small room, and gestured for them to exit before saying, "Well, then I'll send one of the guards down to watch over you two and ensure you behave. And don't protest, Stone. I know exactly what it feels like to finally kiss your bride and not claim her yet. Even those of us with the best self-control have trouble."

He glanced at Reika and her flushed cheeks, and resisted a groan. Because, yes, he wanted to pull her close and kiss her again. "Fine." He waited for Reika to leave the room first before following.

Once they were in the kitchen and Leo had gone upstairs, Reika handed him a frilly white apron. He shook his head. "This isn't what the kitchen staff wear."

She grinned. "Nope. But it's the biggest one I could

find from the former cook. And you're the lucky guy who gets to wear it."

He sighed, put on the white apron, complete with gathered frill things he didn't know the name off, and tied it. As soon as it was on, Reika laughed.

And laughed.

And laughed some more.

He growled. "It's not that amusing."

It took her a second to catch her breath. "But it really is. It's like someone combined a maid character with a grumpy secret service agent, and you were the result. I know: Maid Undercover—eradicating dust like he used to do with terrorists. It could be a comedy and be amazing."

She started laughing again. Even if Stone had no bloody idea what she was talking about—some of the words made no sense—he couldn't help but smile.

Something about Reika's laughter was infectious.

When she finally managed to control herself, she took a deep breath and lightly hit his arm with her fingers. "Well, come on then. I have my second wind right now, and it won't last. And trust me, I'm even grumpier when I'm tired than when I'm hungry."

He grunted, pointed at himself, and raised an eyebrow.

Reika snorted. "Right, what was I thinking? You have grumpy down to an art form."

He was about to say there was a reason for it, but thankfully one of the kitchen maids asked Reika a question and Stone was soon washing dishes.

Even if it wasn't his usual duties, it was somehow soothing to wash, rinse, and dry them.

It also gave him a chance to watch Reika as she interacted with the staff. Unlike the previous cook, she was friendly, constantly thanked everyone, and when needed, was firm without being cruel.

The more he observed her, the more he couldn't believe fate had picked her for him. She was so…good-humored. And kind. And of course bloody beautiful.

And for a damaged, scarred, gruff male like himself, she was a type of ambrosia. He wanted to devour her, always. Both her happy energy and, of course, her sweet cunny.

Shaking his head, he finished his task and escorted Reika up to her room. She faded as they walked, tiring, and he nearly offered to carry her.

But they arrived at her room before he could. And aware of the night guard watching him, he resisted kissing her. "Good night, Reika. I'll find you tomorrow."

She lightly touched his arm. "I can't wait."

Once she shut her door, he smiled to himself. No female had actually wanted to see him again, let alone looked forward to it.

Maybe, just maybe, fate had made a good choice for him.

And he was determined not to fuck it up.

Chapter Six

R eika had been so exhausted the night before that her head had barely hit the pillow before she'd passed out.

The following morning, she woke to sunlight filtering through the curtains. After rolling onto her back, she took a second to think about her new reality.

She wasn't quite sure why finding herself in the past and being torn from everything she'd known had become sort of easy to accept.

Oh, she still wished she could see her mom and stepdad, as well as her coworkers from the bakery.

But she knew she couldn't go back. As was her way, she ignored the depressing stuff to spend more energy on the good stuff.

Such as Stone.

Smiling, she remembered him donning the apron. He'd looked ridiculous in the frilly getup, especially with all his muscles and glares. Almost like a fancy dress costume gone horribly wrong.

And yet, he'd done it and even cracked a smile or two.

Maybe some people would be irritated at his mostly silent nature. However, Reika saw him as a challenge. One that gave her something to focus on instead of worry about.

As the clock on the mantel chimed the hour, she sighed and wondered how the meeting with the fae witch Dark Lord would go.

Finally getting herself out of bed, she rang for a maid to help her with the ridiculous amount of layers and buttons used in this time period.

Before too long, she sat inside the main parlor in the family side of Leo's casino building, the one used to welcome guests.

As she sipped her tea and ate scones, Yesenia waltzed in and sat next to her. After nabbing her own treat, she said, "I heard you and Stone were making out last night. Is that true?"

She resisted groaning. "I'm about to meet this powerful fae witch guy who'll decide my future, and all you want to hear about is me kissing Stone?"

Yesenia waved a hand in dismissal. "Khan's not that bad. He looks scarier than he is. Be respectful but honest, and things should be fine. Especially if you negotiate with him. As much as he complains about it, he likes a challenge." Yesenia leaned forward. "So?"

For a beat, it was hard for Reika to believe this fae witch female—who was only a few years older than herself—had one of the most powerful types of magic. But even if she'd just met Yesenia, it felt as if she could tell her anything. So she blurted, "Yes, it happened. Although your husband stopped us before things got too intense."

Yesenia sighed. "He said he was going to do that. Leo really can be a killjoy at times." She eyed Reika a beat. "So does the kiss mean you'll let Stone claim you once? Maybe even more than once?"

"Once, yes. I don't want him to go insane. After that? I don't know. I need to learn more about him before thinking of the future."

Yesenia nodded. "That's fair. I only know bits and pieces about Stone, thanks to Leo, but it's not my story to share. But regardless of how short a time you've known him, you've already done that man a world of good. I wish it was easier to take pictures in this time because I'm dying to see Stone in a frilly apron."

Reika smiled. "It was super funny. He even smiled for a few seconds."

Yesenia placed a hand over her heart and put on a mock expression of horror. "No, not a smile!" She relaxed. "But truthfully, that's huge for him, for sure."

She was about to ask Yesenia if she could share anything personal about Stone, or even just why he liked to grunt all the time, when there was a knock on the door. Leo entered, closely followed by a male she didn't know.

He had black hair, medium-brown skin, and a stern look on his face. The pointed ears peeking out from his hair confirmed he was a fae witch. However, the way his dark brown eyes studied her, as if trying to figure her out, put her on guard.

To her surprise, the unknown male moved to stand near the fireplace, more than two meters away, instead of sitting in the chair across from her and Yesenia.

Before she could wonder too much about that, Leo spoke. "Miss Reika Hashimoto, may I introduce you to the fae witch Dark Lord, William Khan. Khan, this is Reika Hashimoto, our latest arrival from the twenty-first century and the fated bride of my head of security."

She nodded. "It's nice to meet you, sir."

Yesenia murmured, "Addressing him as Dark Lord is better."

Khan shrugged. "Either will do." He stared at a Reika a second before adding, "From what Yates has told me, you're aware that you can't return to your time." She bobbed her head, and he continued, "Then you essentially have two options: leave with me to live in the fae witch territory, or stay here for the next two weeks to see if you and the half-vampire suit. Either way, you can't remain here long-term without marrying him."

She blinked. "Marry him?"

Yesenia sighed. "Khan, really, this again? First with me, then my brother, and now Reika. Two weeks is super fast and not enough time to make a life-altering decision. Maybe if you were married, you'd understand."

Khan brushed some invisible dirt off his sleeve. "You are well aware, Yesenia, of how things operate here. But I'll elaborate for Miss Hashimoto." His dark-eyed gaze met hers again. "Unlike in the future, we have our respective territories for a reason. Until recently, there was a great deal of war, and retaliation, and lives lost. The territories allow us to protect our own. And even if relations have improved, there is bad blood between the vampires and fae witches. Me allowing any fae witch to live in the vampire's territory without a husband, wife, or committed poly-pairing makes my people uneasy. To keep them from doing anything rash—such as an ill-planned rescue attempt—I have strict rules in place. Marriage is a serious step, so if a fae witch takes it with a vampire, my people understand they wish to live here." He paused, and then asked, "Do you understand?"

So basically, marriage was super important in 1890. "Someone could be forced, though, into marriage. The reasoning seems silly to me."

Khan didn't bat an eye at her words. "Whilst I make the rules, I only do so for a reason, and the two options still stand. Are you leaving with me today? Or will you stay here for the next two weeks to see if this half-vampire suits you?"

Reika glanced at Yesenia, hoping there was another way. However, as the female smiled at her in sympathy, no doubt having gone through something similar herself, Reika knew the Dark Lord was being serious.

Even though she'd only been here a day—a very long day—she was already making friends. Not to mention there was Stone. Between his kisses and getting him to smile, she yearned to know him better. If

Reika left with the Dark Lord today, she knew she'd regret it.

Although marrying the grumpy guy so quickly, without knowing anything about his past, didn't seem like a good solution either.

Then she remembered Yesenia saying that Dark Lord Khan liked a challenge and to negotiate. Sitting taller, she replied, "How about after two weeks, we meet again and discuss if I need more time or not? And I know that's breaking your rules. But I was taken from everything without a word. The very least I deserve is time to better know Stone and what my life might be like with him."

Khan studied her for a minute, and then another. Leo sighed, but Khan spoke before the vampire Dark Lord could. "Perhaps. But I will need convincing. Send me a note if you come up with a good reason. Otherwise, my terms will stand and you'll have two weeks."

Maybe it was Stone's influence already, but Reika wanted to growl.

Yesenia gently squeezed her hand before asking the Dark Lord, "Are you going to place restrictions on her magic? I'm not sure why you would, though, as it's not like mine, meaning it's not super dangerous. But regardless, she has a right to know."

Khan shook his head. "No, I won't place restrictions unless Miss Hashimoto has any secondary powers I should know about?"

It was rare for half-fae witches to have more than one power, and Reika was no different. "No, Dark

Lord Khan. Just the ability to improve the taste of stuff."

"Well, then, feel free to use it. Everyone knows that Yates needed a better cook anyway. His former one was atrocious."

Leo frowned. "I didn't ask for your opinion."

"Clearly."

Reika jumped back in. "I have another question."

The two Dark Lords fell silent, and she ignored how her heart beat a little faster at their combined gazes on her. They both nodded for her to continue. "I know I can't go back to the future, but is there a way to send a note to my mom and stepdad?"

Khan replied, "Maybe. But not until after you decide what to do about Stone Riley."

She could push, but Reika didn't want to irritate Khan just yet.

The fae witch male moved toward the door. "Our meeting is over. I'll have someone visit to check in on you, and a tracker to verify your powers. If you decide to marry the vampire, let me know. I trust Yates to take care of you in the meantime."

The two Dark Lords exited, and Reika sighed. "It's difficult not saying whatever I want."

Yesenia shrugged. "Trust me, I get it. I'm lucky because my husband is a Dark Lord, so I have more leeway. But at least the paranormals are more open-minded than the humans in this time period. Shitty doesn't even begin to cover what human females have to put up with." Yesenia stood. "Now that's over, let's go visit the kitchen and then track down Stone. You don't have a lot of time to decide your future, so you'd better make the most of it."

Reika nodded and followed the fae witch out of the room.

She'd never been one to make hasty decisions since her father's—when he'd gone on an impulsive run through an illegal hunting ground used by humans—had killed him. However, she didn't have much choice this time. Because no matter what she decided, it'd be a bit hasty.

The best she could do was convince Stone to spend as much time with her as possible. And if there was one thing that usually worked with males, it was food. If she could discover his favorites, then she'd make him something unique but tasty.

However, she wanted it to taste amazing but look awful. Because then he might react and show some emotion again. Maybe they'd even laugh about her trick afterward.

And despite knowing him a short time, Reika knew that Stone definitely needed more fun and laughter in his life.

Chapter Seven

Stone stared down at the questionable-looking bowl of food and frowned. "What the bloody hell is this supposed to be?"

Amusement danced in Reika's eyes. "Dinner."

The brown mush looked more like shite than food. "Is this what they eat in the future?"

She shrugged one shoulder. "Maybe, maybe not. Try it and I'll tell you."

He raised his brows. "If this is actually horse shite, then I'm tempted to lay you over my lap and smack your arse."

As soon as the words left his mouth, he regretted them. From what he could gather, nice females didn't like that sort of thing.

But Reika merely rose to her toes and down again. "Now I wish it was horse crap."

Heat rushed through Stone's body and straight to his cock. "What?"

She leaned closer and whispered, "I'm open to a little ass-smacking if you are."

He nearly dropped the bowl in his hands.

She laughed. "You can close your mouth, Stone, before a fly buzzes in."

He did and frowned at her. "Are all females from the future so bold?"

"I have no idea. But we only have two weeks, remember? So I'm trying to be myself, without the walls and politeness I use with strangers. Plus, for me, sex is a crucial part of a relationship. I might be great friends with a guy, but if he can't be bothered to ensure I orgasm too, then he's not a future I want. My shifter half would never be content, even if it's not dominant. Aren't you the same way? Don't you want to find out all this stuff now?"

For a few beats, all Stone could do was stare at the short fae witch and the truth in her gaze. He could easily imagine her refusing a male for being lazy and inattentive.

That wouldn't be problem for him, of course. Ever since he'd kissed her, Stone had thought of nothing but making her scream his name as she orgasmed around his cock.

Putting aside his daydreams, being more honest about sex was important, given his past. Especially since Stone needed to be mostly in control. Not completely, but enough to wipe away memories of when he'd had no free will.

Part of him wanted to tell Reika everything, the good and bad, about his life. However, something held him back. His past wasn't pretty, and he didn't want to scare her off so early.

Eventually he would say or reveal something to send her fleeing. No female in his life had ever stuck around.

But he was a selfish bastard and wanted to absorb more of her happy nature for a bit longer.

Oh, and take in her slight curves and extremely kissable lips.

Before he could stop himself, he stared at her mouth. And then the vixen licked her lips.

Stone nearly groaned. He'd rather eat her for dinner than the mush in his bowl.

Not yet. Once he drank from her and tasted her blood, it would only get harder and harder to hold back and not try to claim her. And she was right—they needed to be a little more familiar before he could claim her with his fangs and cock.

But then she laid a hand on his arm and leaned closer, enveloping him with her sweet feminine scent mixed with the spices from the kitchen.

Fuck, he wanted to devour her from head to toe.

She took the spoon from his fingers, scooped up the mush, and held it out to him. "Try it and then we can have the next course."

His voice was hoarse to his own ears when he asked, "What's the next course?"

She smiled slowly. "Me."

Bloody hell. Was she indeed real?

As she waggled the spoon near his mouth, he closed his lips around it and never broke his gaze. As soon as it touched his tongue, a savory, decadent flavor filled his mouth. There was definitely beef and potatoes and some sort of vegetable.

He moaned. Whatever it was, it was fucking delicious.

Reika took the spoon back, wiped the corner of his mouth with her thumb, and then sucked it into her mouth. Without thinking, he blurted, "I'm jealous of your finger."

She released it with a pop, licked her lips, and Stone lost control.

Quickly placing the bowl on the nearby table, he hauled her body against his and kissed her.

Her lips parted instantly, and he caressed, and licked, and explored every inch of her mouth, loving how she met him stroke for stroke. When she started rubbing against him, Stone lifted her and sat her on the table, spreading her legs as much as he could with her skirts before moving into the space between.

When he broke the kiss, he nibbled her jaw, her ear —taking time to lightly tease the points which made her cry out—and then slowly tortured her with nips and licks where her neck met her shoulder. Her pulse thundered, calling to him, making his fangs ache to pierce her soft flesh.

"Stone," she murmured and then pulled his head back up to kiss her.

He cupped her cheek with one hand and used the other to pull up her skirts. Once they were at her waist, he moved to stand closer, until her wet, hot cunt pressed against his aching trouser-clad cock.

Leave it to his fae witch to be naughty and not wear underthings.

Fuck. It wouldn't take much to undo his trousers and slide right into her.

But then his conscience niggled at the back of his mind. Was she an innocent?

If so, she deserved better than a quick tupping on a table in the small parlor.

Breaking the kiss, he laid his forehead against hers and took a second to catch his breath.

Reika asked breathlessly, "Why did you stop?"

"You deserve better than me fucking you on a table."

She ran a hand down the front of his chest, lingering to play with the buttons on his waistcoat. Each small movement made him want to groan.

She had a bloody magical touch, that was for sure.

"Look at me, Stone." Once he did, she searched his eyes and lightly traced his cheek. "This is usually something I'd share later, but as I mentioned before, we're pressed for time. In the future, virginity isn't such a huge thing. I've been with males before."

At first, jealousy and anger coursed through him. He didn't like the thought of another male touching her.

But then the truth of her words sank in—he wouldn't have to try to be slow and gentle, two things that weren't in his nature at all.

He liked it fast, and hard, and intense. That was the opposite of what he'd had to endure during his ten years as a slave.

Although imagining Reika naked and tied to their bed as he slowly kissed every inch of her body didn't turn him off. If anything, his cock turned harder.

Maybe with her, he didn't have to worry about the past or what had been, but rather could just live in the moment and enjoy it.

Maybe the right person changed everything.

Reika cupped his cheek. "Okay, talk to me. And yes, I know, you're not Mr. Chatty. But I didn't like the look that just flashed into your eyes. Tell me what's wrong."

He searched her dark brown eyes. The concern there unleashed a longing he'd never had before—to not hold back and hope the person wouldn't reject him.

"Stone, please. Just tell me."

Stepping back, he pulled down her skirt. Reika frowned, but he spoke before she could. "This isn't something I can do with your cunny on display."

She tilted her head and closed her legs. "So you'll tell me what you were thinking about?"

He nodded, put out a hand, and she took it. Once he helped her down and eased her into the chair, he sat on the opposite side of the small table. If he was to get through this, then he couldn't risk her trying to touch and comfort him.

He cleared his throat. "I may lose my voice from talking so much, but I'll try to get through this." She smiled briefly but then gestured for him to get going.

It looked like he was going to fucking do this.

Staring a second at Reika and getting lost in her eyes, he found the courage to start. "My mother was a whore who sold me at age nine to an illegal fight ring master."

She gasped, and Stone looked away to the flame of one of the candles. Doing his best to keep the memories at bay, he continued, "She was a drunkard, and I was just something she could use to earn money. I was good at begging when I was little, but by nine, I was getting too old to get much sympathy, let alone coin.

"And my father was one of her clients, someone who wanted nothing to do with me or her, so there was no assistance or help there. I never cared much as a child that I didn't have a father, or that I had to spend time asking people for food. I just wanted to try and make my mother happy."

Not that it had ever fucking worked.

Her parting words still stung. *"You're a worthless piece of rubbish, Stone. You ruined my life, and I don't know why I kept you all these years. You're a selfish, greedy child who doesn't deserve to be loved. I'll be happier without you, and so that's what I'm doing, abandoning you like I should've done nine years ago."*

Not wanting to remember how lost and sad he'd been to see his mother leave him with the fight ring master, he focused back on telling Reika what she needed to know. "Growing up, it was the other females in the brothel who looked after me, more than my own mother did.

"But despite their kindness, they all had their own worries. So even if they knew my mother was going to sell me, it wasn't as if they had the means to do anything about it."

One of the prostitutes, Mary, had been more a mother to him than his own. She'd told him to be brave and fight to stay alive. Because one day, she knew he'd be able to do something with his life. She had a feeling.

Not that he'd ever been able to tell her what he'd eventually accomplished. No, she'd died shortly after he left.

A glass of water slid toward him, pulling him back to the present. "In case you need it," Reika said.

He took a sip, cleared his throat, and continued. "I was sold to a male who used me as a boy fighter until I started to grow too tall. He liked to run invite-only fights between boys aged eight to eleven, and then sometimes matches between gangly teens. His customers liked the unpredictability of who might win, and placed bets on us."

Anger flashed in her gaze. "The assholes."

He smiled at her attempt at cursing. "I agree. However, I was one of the lucky ones—I survived. But then at fourteen, he sold me to a human couple who wanted a vampire plaything. Even if I'm only half, they couldn't tell. They were addicted to a vampire's bite and wanted a constant source at hand."

Not for the first time Stone cursed the fact a vampire's fangs secreted a substance that instantly brought on an orgasm.

He'd been used on demand for so long he'd grown to hate biting anyone. Once he'd been free, he'd relied on drinking from a cup for nearly a decade before he could handle being near someone's flesh again.

Tracing the rim of the glass, he pushed on. "For the

next ten years, I had no free will. I wasn't even allowed to speak unless one of them gave permission." He finally met her gaze, ignoring the surprise there. "They did whatever they wanted with me. Anything and everything."

Understanding flashed in her eyes, and then fire. "Who would do that to a child?"

Part of him wanted to laugh at her naïvety. However, he remembered that she didn't know how nineteenth century England worked. "Back then, decades ago, it was considered fashionable to own a paranormal, especially once buying human slaves became illegal. However, to appease those in power, the government turned a blind eye to people still buying and owning paranormals."

Reika growled. "Bastards."

He nodded. "It's at least a little better now, especially in London. The head of the Metropolitan Police made it a priority to arrest those trading in paranormals. They have to be far more secretive now to get away with it."

He could see she wanted to ask questions, but Stone needed to stop stalling and share arguably the worst part of his past, the part that might drive her away.

But Reika deserved to know the full truth before she spent any more time with him.

So he spoke before she could. "Let's go back to the couple who owned me, and well, they became more and more addicted to my bite. Eventually, I was able to use that weakness against them and obtain my freedom."

"How?"

"By staging their deaths to look like an accident."

Reika turned pale. "You killed them?"

He met her gaze head-on. Stone wouldn't lie about this, even if he could. She deserved the truth. "Yes. And I'd do it again without hesitation."

He waited to see how the sweet, happy fae witch would react. Stone had never killed since, unless it was during a battle. However, he would never regret pushing the orgasm-drunk couple into the lake and letting them drown.

As Reika listened to Stone reveal one horrible thing after another, she simultaneously wanted to cry and hit something. Him not being able to talk freely, let alone be in control of what was done to him, revealed why Stone was the way he was.

Yesenia had warned her about the nineteenth century being more violent and dangerous, but it'd all been in the abstract. However, listening to Stone's tale, it suddenly made her appreciate how boring and safe the future had been by comparison, even with all its faults.

But as soon as he admitted to murdering the couple who'd bought him, she froze.

He didn't regret it either. And for a second, she tried to imagine being in his shoes, living the same life of slavery and exploitation, and wondered if she would've done the same if it meant gaining her freedom?

Reika honestly didn't know. Although if she had lived ten years without ever being able to make a choice, she probably would've thought of a million ways to try and kill those who controlled her.

Stone sat impassive, staring at her, no doubt waiting to see if she'd flee from the room, shout at him, or basically tell him she didn't want anything to do with him.

But something about this male, this strong half-vampire with such a dark past, called to her. Reika had always tried to find the good in everything. It was merely how she lived life to the fullest each day.

However, she knew not everyone could do that, or cope the same way. And if she had lived Stone's life, she probably would be a lot less cheery, and chatty, and unused to being teased.

The thought of being the one to help him see the good in life, the laughter, the ability to open up and not think people would abandon you, or sell you, or some other horrible thing, clinched how she would respond.

Well, after she had one more answer, at any rate. Condoning murder to escape hell was one thing, but doing it willy-nilly was another.

She propped her elbows on the table and asked, "Did you kill anyone else, apart from the couple who abused you?"

He frowned a beat, looking at her like he couldn't believe she was still in the same room, and finally replied, "I've taken a few other lives since then, but only in self-defense. I went on a rescue mission with Leo earlier this year, to retrieve his kidnapped nephew, and I had to kill someone who was trying to kill me first."

The fact he was so honest and upfront erased her lingering doubts.

Reika nodded, moved a hand to lay it on the table, palm up, and stated, "Then I'm not giving up yet, Stone. Self-defense and wanting to escape slavery and abuse are reasons I understand for why you did what you did. I'm not sure I could ever do it myself, although I'll never know for sure until the moment happens. However, it doesn't make me hate you, or despise you, or anything like that." She wiggled her fingers. "I have a feeling you're not used to comfort, but I want to give you a little. No one's here to see if we hold hands."

It was an innocent, almost middle-school type thing to suggest. And yet, she didn't want to brush past this important moment. Yes, she wanted him to kiss her again like before, but if she was going to marry him, there needed to be more than lust and sex. She wanted to connect on so many more levels, and somehow she sensed Stone wanted it even more than her.

After what seemed like an hour but was probably only a minute, he placed his much larger, rougher hand in hers.

Ignoring the spark that traveled up her arm at his touch, Reika curled her fingers around his and squeezed. "See? The world didn't end." She lowered her voice dramatically. "You could even smile, and no one would ever know."

His lips twitched, and so Reika shook her head. "Not good enough. Where's that smile I know is dying to get out? The one that makes you so sexy?"

He did grin then and the sight made her heart warm. "You're bloody ridiculous at times."

She shrugged. "Sometimes life needs to be a little ridiculous. It helps us cope with all the hard times, or sad things, or insert awful thing here." She knew she couldn't completely blow past what he'd revealed, so Reika did her best to be serious. "As for what you shared with me, I'll admit I was shocked at first. But I understand why you did what you did. I can't even imagine being owned and controlled against my will for that long. However, the most important thing is that you survived, Stone." She squeezed his hand again. "And if you ever need someone to talk to about it, I'm around. I promise to always listen and take in what you say without judgement."

He searched her gaze, and she waited to see if he'd believe her or not. Because his answer would determine their future.

DESPITE BEING NEARLY fifty years old, Stone had never sat and held someone's hand before.

Oh, he'd had sex over the years, to slake his shifter half's craving for sex. But it'd been quick and fairly impersonal. As soon as they'd finished, they'd parted. There had never been a need for more.

And not even when he'd been a boy living in the brothel had his mother or Mary showed him much affection. The only hug he could remember had been when Mary had said goodbye to him.

And yet, Reika's much smaller hand squeezing his did something to his heart that he wanted to ignore.

Stone Riley didn't do softness or gentleness. And honestly, he'd never dreamed of being worth someone's time or affection.

And now? The fae witch who'd made his heart beat again made him want things he'd never dared dream of before.

Then she offered to listen to him anytime, anywhere, and he saw nothing but honesty in her eyes.

With anyone else, he'd scoff. But with this female from the future? He didn't want to do that. No, he could easily imagine having conversations with her instead of glaring, and grunting, and trying to scare people off.

And he vowed right then and there to be honest with her, no matter how difficult it might be. "Thank you. Sharing anything with others is new. But the fact you offered to listen, knowing my past isn't a happy one, shows how understanding and brilliant you are."

She grinned, and Stone stopped breathing. Not only was Reika kind, positive, and sometimes amusing, she was also so bloody beautiful. She replied, "Well, as much as the sexy, broody version of Stone caught my attention, this honest, hand-holding version is way better."

He grunted, unsure of how to reply to that. Emotions weren't his forte.

After squeezing his hand one last time, she released it, and he nearly reached for her but somehow restrained himself.

Reika fetched the mushed-filled bowls and placed one in front of him. "Eat. And then we're going to do something fun. And no, not the hot and bothered version. At least not tonight. Date night first. Hot and sweaty times later."

He raised his brows. "Date night? What's that?"

"What do you call it in this time period? Courting, I think? But not quite so formal. I want to play a game, or cards, or something fun. How you win or lose will tell me a whole lot about you."

He shook his head. "I don't lose at cards."

She winked. "We'll see."

As they finished their meal, Reika mostly chatted about the bakery she'd worked for in the future, and Stone relaxed. At one point he laughed when she told the story of how a giant bag of flour had split open when she moved it, covering her and everyone else in white. But instead of getting mad, she'd merely said, "Boo," like a ghost.

She really was special—a light he desperately wanted to hold close, to absorb her heat and energy, and use as a constant balm on his soul.

Of course then they played cards, some game he'd never heard of before, and he lost.

His growly self had returned, but a few words from Reika, and he'd been smiling again.

After walking her to her door and saying goodnight, Stone couldn't stop grinning until he fell asleep.

Maybe he could hope for happiness, or even love, after all.

Chapter Eight

The next morning, Reika hummed as she cleaned up the kitchen after breakfast and counted down the minutes until she saw Stone again.

Something had changed between them the night before, she was sure of it.

The only downside had been not kissing him goodnight. However, she'd wanted some distance between him revealing his past and her all but jumping him. He'd not only been fragile, but she also didn't want him thinking she'd slept with him out of pity or high emotions.

No, she wanted Stone for himself, and she needed him to know that.

Crazy as it was, she was already falling for him.

Reika had just finished tidying up the tables when one of the kitchen maids—Ida, who'd been hired right after the old cook had stormed out—rushed in. "Oh, miss, thank goodness I found you. There's a delivery but I can't find the housekeeper anywhere."

Reika was about to ask if the cook usually accepted deliveries here or not, but held back. It was hard enough getting some of the kitchen staff to listen to her, what with her being a foreigner from the future.

Besides, during her time at the bakery, she'd often had to accept orders if the owner hadn't been around.

Tossing her towel aside, she took off her apron and nodded. "Take me to them, and I'll handle it."

The maid bobbed and gestured for Reika to follow.

They walked down the winding downstairs corridor, further and further, until she frowned. "Isn't the main door for this floor back there?"

"Yes, miss. But some of the deliveries use the other door because it's easier to get their heavy loads closer to the building."

She wasn't sure what to make of the reasoning, especially as the hallway became even narrower.

But they reached the door before Reika could think of turning back, and the maid opened it. A man in slightly dirty clothes and a worn hat stood there, a piece of paper in his hands. "I have the gin delivery here, miss. I just need you to come inspect the cart."

Reika looked over the man's shoulder. A number of males stood near it, all of them standing in the bright sunshine without flinching. Their ears were normal, too, without points. Which meant they were either shifter, half vampire, or human.

Even if the British shifters and vampires had a

truce, Reika didn't like how they eyed her with interest. Too much interest.

She cleared her throat and did her best to put some authority into her voice. "The butler is in charge of all the alcohol, and should handle this. I'll go get him."

Reika tried to step backward, but Ida had moved behind her. Any friendliness had vanished as the maid spit out, "This is for getting my aunt sacked, you bloody, dirty foreigner."

She shoved. Hard. And Reika stumbled.

Right into the hands of the man at the door.

She opened her mouth to scream, but a cloth was instantly pressed against her face. And as the world dimmed, she wished she'd been more careful, just like Stone had advised.

Stone. Her last thought was maybe he could find her before it was too late. And if he did, she'd follow his orders to the letter in the future.

STONE HAD AGREED to meet Reika for luncheon.

But as he checked his pocket watch and saw it was only half nine, he didn't care if it was hours too early. He needed to see her again. Whether for good or bad, he was slowly becoming addicted to her silliness and laughter. Something he'd lacked his entire life.

However, as soon as he reached the stairs leading down to the kitchen and servant area, he ran into the housekeeper, Mrs. Green.

At her flushed cheeks and fear-filled blue eyes, he went on high alert. "What's wrong, Mrs. Green?"

"It's Miss Hashimoto. She was taken."

His heart skipped a beat. "What?"

The housekeeper wrung her hands. "There was a delivery, and she went to approve it, so Betsy told me. But no one's seen her since."

Doing his best to tamp down his panic—because if something had happened to her, it'd kill a piece of him inside—Stone concentrated on getting information. "Then how do you know she was taken?"

The housekeeper reached into her pocket, took out a handkerchief, and unfolded it. Inside were large chunks of black, shiny hair.

Hair that looked a lot like Reika's.

Only because of his years of working security for Leo could he calmly take the handkerchief from Mrs. Green and study it.

There wasn't any blood, which was a good sign. And it had been cut or sliced, not torn out. But he needed a lot more than this if he was to find her.

And he would find her. Because even if he had to tear apart the entire East End of London, he'd bloody well do it to find his fated bride. "What else do you know?"

"Well, one of the kitchen maids is also missing— Ida Smith. No one's seen her since breakfast." Mrs. Green held out a folded piece of paper. "A stable lad found this behind one of the barrels near the door, and thought it might be important."

He took it and noted it was an invoice. The name

of the shop was unfamiliar, and since Stone knew every merchant who dealt with the Fated Wheel—he was in charge of investigating them prior to signing any contracts—it was probably fake.

A fake merchant, a missing kitchen maid, and hacked off hair. His gut said he was missing something important, a vital piece that could tell him where to start looking, but what?

Just as he was about to ask Mrs. Green to move aside so he could interrogate the kitchen staff, the butler came up the stairs with a pale, blonde-haired maid in tow. She was one of the new ones, Meg, if he remembered right.

The butler nodded at him and said, "Meg here has something to tell you."

Stone did his best not to glare. "What is it?"

She swallowed. "I-I overheard something earlier. I was fetching some supplies for the cook in the small room furthest down the hall. But as soon as I heard Ida discussing what to do with Miss Hashimoto, I hid, afraid for my life."

Part of him wanted to roar that she could've stopped Reika's kidnapping. But after really looking at the female, who couldn't be more than sixteen, his more rational side won out. "Just tell us what you heard, Meg. That's all I care about."

She swallowed, looked at the housekeeper, who gave an encouraging nod, and then finally answered, "A male mentioned a gin delivery, and then Ida said something about Miss Hashimoto deserved to be punished for what she did to her aunt. I think she was related to the former cook, although I never met her, so I don't know nothing about her."

Ida had been one of the hastily hired kitchen maids. Despite Stone's warnings, Leo had waved aside the usual checks into potential staff, saying he needed a functioning kitchen for his gaming hell.

Stone clenched the fingers of one hand into a fist. If Reika was harmed or killed because of the rush, he might just have to challenge the Dark Lord himself.

He must've growled because Meg shrank into herself. Mrs. Green patted the girl's arm. "Stone won't hurt you, Meg. Is there anything else you heard or remember?"

"O-only that I heard a male voice, and he mentioned others waiting outside. But that's it, Mrs. Green, I swear."

Once he nodded for the housekeeper to take Meg away, he turned toward the butler, Mr. Jameson. "I'll need help searching the area near the smaller back door. Send me any half-vampires you can spare for the job. And if they find anything, I'll be interviewing some of the local runner lads, flower seller girls, and others working on the street who might've seen something."

The butler nodded. "I'll get it sorted right away."

Since Stone and Jameson had worked together for years, Stone didn't have to remind the butler to keep Leo in the loop.

As Stone walked toward the rear door, anger churned in his belly. Under normal circumstances, he'd probably talk with Leo first.

However, he wasn't going to waste any more time,

not when Reika's life was at stake. He'd vowed to protect her, and he was bloody well going to do it. No matter what.

After walking into the bright morning light, Stone scouted the area and headed toward the boy selling papers. With each step, he pushed down his fear and dread of what might've happened to her.

No. Reika was still alive. She had to be.

And now, well, now it was time to save his female. And once she was safe, he'd fucking make sure the bastard who'd taken her would regret it forever.

Chapter Nine

Reika woke up in a dark, windowless room, the only light coming from an oil lantern propped on a large wooden crate.

As she tried to sit up, she noticed her hands were tied tightly in front of her with rope, to the point she could barely feel her fingers.

The moldy smell, the sound of scratching—probably from rats—and the male laughter outside her door made her heart race.

Then she remembered—the delivery, the maid blocking her way, and being grabbed before the world went black. And judging by the room she was in and her bindings, she was now a prisoner.

And she had no idea what they'd do to her.

Fear danced up her spine. Because if they had wanted to merely kill her, she'd be dead already. Which meant they had plans. Ones that probably wouldn't end well.

She struggled to breathe as images flashed of torture and rape and who knew what else.

No, Reika. Stop it. She couldn't fall apart. She *wouldn't* fall apart.

Taking a deep breath, she tried to calm her heart a fraction. Maybe someday she could laugh about everything. After all, never in a million years would she have expected a cook to get revenge by kidnapping the new hire, and then doing who knew what to her. It was like a bad movie or something.

The sound of tiny claws drew closer, reminding her of where she was, and Reika backed up further against the wall. She hated rats and spiders. And as the sounds of tiny claws continued to scratch against wood, she wondered if the rats would eat and eventually kill her.

Her heart pounded harder, but then Stone's strong, tall image flashed into her mind. Would he be looking for her already? Because from everything she'd heard, he was pretty good at finding lost people, or rescuing those who needed it. The housekeeper had done nothing but sing his praises.

But how in the world would he even know where to start looking for her? Unless someone had seen her being taken, they might just think she'd left on her own. Especially since she doubted Ida had stuck around to be questioned.

Maybe she'd die in this place after all.

Her eyes heated with tears, but she shook her head. *No, no crying. Be strong and see if you can save yourself. You don't want to be the stupid chick in the movie who thinks freaking out will help. Look around the room and see what you can do to get your hands free. You can do this.*

After a few more deep breaths, some of her fear receded, and Reika's mind started to work again.

Her eyes had adjusted to the dim light, and she studied the room more closely. Wooden crates, in a variety of sizes, littered the small space. Some were open, others not, and several of the lids were propped against the wall.

Thanking the stupidity of her kidnappers for not tying up her feet, she slowly walked over to the open crates, careful to make as little noise as possible.

Even if the containers were empty, some of the lids sat haphazardly propped against the wall. She noticed a long nail sticking out of one of them.

If she could cut through the rope on her wrists, then maybe she could use some of the crate lids as a type of weapon.

She might not be able to win against the large number of males she'd seen back at the cart. However, she wasn't about to cower and simply let them kill her —let alone rape her—without a fight and maybe taking one of them down with her.

This, right here, was one of those situations Reika had never imagined being in—planning how to survive even if it meant harming or killing another.

And yet, despite the odds against her, she desperately wanted to fight and try to live for so many reasons. To be able to let her mother know she was safe, to do her best to run a business in this time period, and of course, to kiss Stone, hold him close, and make him laugh while they were naked in bed.

She simply had too much unfinished business, and she needed to try and escape some way, somehow.

Reika went to the crate lid with the nail and maneuvered to the floor, all without knocking anything over. As she sawed at her ropes, hoping she was up to date on her tetanus shots in case she cut herself, she still willed for Stone to find her. She was all for fighting for her best chance, but she would most likely need help if she were to get out of this situation alive.

However, the best she could do was be less of a weakness if Stone did find her. And so, despite the ache in her shoulders and the mind-numbingly slow progress on cutting the rope, Reika kept at it. She wasn't about to let a disgruntled cook ruin the future she could see on the horizon.

STONE DID his best to ignore the stench coming from the brick building and its large, mostly empty yard.

Thanks to Old Tom—one of the corner costermongers who hawked his wares to the cooks and households near Leo's gaming hell—Stone had learned about the wagon with five males and a female slumped against one of them. The cart had stood out to Tom because it carried bottles of alcohol, and those deliveries were always done later in the day along his route.

Stone had then followed the progress of the bottle-carrying wagon by questioning the children, shopkeepers, flower sellers, or anyone who might've noticed it. The information had finally led him here, to the yard of the night soil men.

He barely paid any notice to the reek of shite and piss. No, he and several of his trusted guards from Leo's place were watching and waiting for the best time to strike.

Because once the cart with the slumped female had reached this building, it hadn't been seen by anyone further down the road. And since one of the local lads had noticed it drive into this yard—it was a far nicer cart than the usual night soil men—it meant Reika had to be inside.

Not wanting to think they'd killed and buried her in the land outside London where the employees deposited their loads of waste, he focused on weaknesses in the building's security and how to sneak inside.

Since it was dark, the night soil carts had already left to collect refuse from the homes without flushing toilets. Which meant there should be fewer people to deal with, making it a better time to act.

As he ran through a number of possibilities, his most trusted fellow guard, Theo, approached and whispered, "One of the maids said that only a handful of workers would still be inside at this time of night. She'd also been given a strange instruction—to stay away from the storage rooms. Somewhere she usually went on a regular basis, to fetch cleaning supplies."

Stone grunted at his friend. Dark-skinned with a

winning smile, Theo was good at charming females to get what he wanted. No doubt he'd used his hands and mouth to convince the maid, but Stone wouldn't judge. If the female wanted a quick tup, then it wasn't his business. "Right, then combined with what else we know, we go with the plan we made earlier."

Theo nodded and went to inform the others.

It seemed forever before he heard the bird call signal that said everyone was in position. Stone withdrew his knife, ensured his pistol would be easy to draw if needed, and counted to one hundred. He gave his own bird whistle, and they all quietly, and slowly, snuck up to the rear entrance, the one usually used by the servants or the night soil men themselves.

Stone allowed Theo to pick the lock, and the other male gently pushed the door inward. Assured the hinges were well-oiled and wouldn't squeak, Theo opened it fully.

After a quick look, Theo motioned for them to proceed. Stone took the lead, and once they all were inside with the door shut, he listened closely.

There. While faint, male laughter came from further down the hall, maybe even from downstairs. Any sort of group in the building wouldn't be employees, not at this time of night.

After gesturing for everyone to follow, they all moved toward the sound. Once they stopped in front of the closed door, a male voice could be heard from the other side as he said, "How much longer do we have to wait? I've never fucked a bitch from the Far East, and I'm ready to welcome her to London and show her what real males can do."

Stone barely heard the laughter as anger churned in his stomach. There was no fucking way he'd let those arseholes touch Reika. And for that insult, he'd make sure they suffered.

Theo laid a hand on his arm and leaned closer to whisper softly, "Calm the fuck down. We won't move until you do."

Taking a deep breath, Stone nodded, getting a grip on his anger. He could unleash it on the bastards once Reika was safe, but not before.

Temper finally reined in, he gave his team a particular series of gestures for the rescue plan. Once done, Theo picked the lock and twisted the handle without pushing it inward. After a few more seconds, Stone gave the signal and Theo opened the door.

It didn't squeak—he silently thanked the servants for doing their jobs—and they descended, the male voices growing louder. Just as one started to describe what he was going to do with Reika's body, Stone motioned for them to attack.

As he rushed toward the males, four startled gazes met his. Stone narrowed his eyes and immediately went after the male trying to draw a pistol.

In a flash, he knocked the weapon from the male's grip and punched him in the nose. When he screamed, Stone then gave an uppercut and the man fell to the ground with a thud.

He turned, ready to take down another bastard, only to discover his men had either contained them or knocked them unconscious. Stone grunted. "That was bloody easy."

One of the still conscious males gave a bloody smile. "Oh, St. Vincent will find you, no doubt."

Stone didn't recognize the name but tucked away the information for later. He approached the male, grabbed his shirt, and lifted him off the ground. "Where is she?"

When he said nothing, Stone kneed the male's groin. He squealed, and Stone shook him. "Tell me where she is or I'll cut off your bollocks next."

The disgusting arsehole squeaked, "She's just in there, behind that door."

After one more shake, he dropped the male into Theo's care and went to the door at the far end of the room. "Reika?"

"Stone?"

At the sound of her voice, relief flooded through him. "Yes, it's me. Give us a minute and we'll get you free."

One of his men handed him a key. As soon as he opened the door, he was bombarded with the smell of mildew and mustiness, to the point it made his eyes water.

And Reika had been trapped inside this place for an entire day. The urge to turn and punch the bastards in the next room was strong. However, as soon as he spotted her tossing aside a piece of wood and shaking, he forgot about anything else but her. After rushing to her, he took her face in his hands and searched her eyes. There was fatigue, and a little fear, but mostly relief.

Thank fuck. She was still alive.

Since he'd never been good with words, Stone pulled her close and crushed his mouth to hers.

REIKA HAD BEEN STANDING in the corner, gripping the length of wood she'd pried from a crate, for what seemed like hours.

As the day drew on, the guys on the other side of the door had become more and more detailed in what they wanted to do to her.

Oh, before they killed her.

It'd taken a lot of inner pep talks to keep herself together, to not give in and cry, or give up all hope.

True, it'd become harder and harder to remain positive as the day had worn on. But she'd refused to surrender, especially once she'd freed her wrists and had a weapon. Then it'd just been a very, very long day of waiting to see if she'd have to fight for her life, or if Stone would find her.

She hated having to rely on someone to rescue her. But the nineteenth century was no joke, and she most definitely needed help to survive it.

When the laughter and crude comments had suddenly died down, followed by grunts and what sounded like punches, Reika pushed aside her fatigue and readjusted her hold on the wood. Her heart raced, all while she tried not to get her hopes up. She wanted it to be Stone, but she couldn't risk lowering her guard.

Not if she wanted to do some damage before finally losing to the four males.

The noises finally stopped and her heart raced. "Reika?"

At the sound of Stone's deep, growly voice, she let out a silent sob.

He'd found her.

Once the door was open, she finally tossed aside the dratted wood and did her best not to faint.

She opened her mouth, but in the next second, Stone pulled her close, cupped her face, and then kissed her.

Relief flooded her as she clung to him, needing to feel his heat, and strength, and the possessive strokes of his tongue.

She may not have known him long, but Stone had become an important part of her life. One that made her feel safe, and wanted, and a million other things she'd never felt with another male.

He gripped her arse and rocked her against him. Reika moaned in pleasure, and he took the kiss deeper.

She had no idea how long they stayed like that— gripping each other like a lifeline, kissing, and both trying to reassure the other that they were alive and things would be okay.

A voice she didn't recognize finally broke through their reunion. "Stone, we need to go. One of the arseholes said their leader will be back soon, and if we want to catch him eventually, we'll need to retreat first. The bastard apparently works with the bloody French vampires."

Reika had no idea what they were talking about, but Stone turned—still keeping an arm about her waist —and asked, "Why would they want Reika?"

The other male shrugged. "Something about how they're funding anything that could hurt or weaken Leo and the London vampire community."

Stone cursed. "Then let's go so we can catch the bastard another day, when we're better prepared. However, we're taking that rubbish with us. They might still be useful."

The male nodded, and Reika opened her mouth, but Stone beat her to it. "I'll explain everything once you're back at my flat and are warm, fed, and safe."

Maybe if she hadn't been kidnapped and held prisoner in a rat-infested room all day, she might've teased him about staying at his place. But she was exhausted, both emotionally and physically, and being held and protected by her big, strong half-vampire, half-shifter male sounded like heaven. "Okay."

He frowned a beat, but then he scooped her into his arms. She squeaked and then stated, "Put me down. I can walk."

"No. You're tired, and I have the route home memorized. It's faster this way."

Too tired to argue, she leaned against him, putting her head on his shoulder. Just being against his warm body made her sleepy, and she yawned. "Fine. But later you're going to explain everything, no matter how long it takes."

He kissed her forehead. "Anything you wish, love."

The endearment might not mean anything, but she

couldn't help smiling up at him. His gaze softened for a beat before he focused on his team and getting back to safer territory.

Before long, they were outside and skulking through the darkness. As he wound through a series of streets, Reika tried her best to stay awake. But his warmth, and the rocking of his body as he walked—as well as the fact she knew he'd keep her safe, no matter what—finally soothed her enough to fall asleep in his arms.

Chapter Ten

Stone had never imagined that merely holding a sleeping female in his arms could make him so happy.

And yet, Reika's soft snores and the heat of her breath across his chest, soothed him in a way nothing else ever had.

His entire body was aware of her softness pressed against him. But holding her, feeling her warmth and knowing she was alive, kept his lust in check.

There would be plenty of time for that once she was awake and recovered. As soon as she said the word, he'd gladly strip her, spread her thighs, and bring her to orgasm with his mouth before claiming her with fangs and cock.

Once would never be enough, though. And no matter what it took, he was going to make her his bride in truth and marry her.

The night before had made that crystal clear to him, when he hadn't know if she was still alive or hurt, or worse.

Only when he'd held Reika in his arms again had a sense of rightness settled over him, calming him, making him think fate was right in that he'd been born for this female and this female alone.

Reika stirred and nuzzled her cheek against his bare chest, bringing him out of his head and sending blood to his cock. Mentally telling the beast to calm the fuck down, he merely stroked Reika's back in slow circles, wishing he could feel her skin instead of the material of her nightgown. When she finally raised her head, he quickly covered his neck with his hand to hide his scar —he'd deal with that revelation later—and her beautiful brown eyes met his. Even with disheveled hair she was still so fucking beautiful. He barely resisted kissing her. "You're awake."

She smiled, and it made it even harder to resist claiming her straight away. "Yep, but I gotta admit, I have the best pillow in the world and am tempted to go back to sleep."

As she laid her head down and rubbed against him, he was too distracted by her touch to notice her hand moving to his side. As her fingers danced across his skin, he yelped.

Raising her head, she laughed. "You *are* ticklish. Now I know how to get you at my mercy."

He caught her hand, brought it to his lips, and kissed her palm. "You have many ways to put me at your mercy, Reika."

For a beat, her eyes blazed with heat. The sight made his bollocks tighten and his cock even harder.

Fuck, he wanted to claim her.

But then he remembered she'd been a prisoner only the day before. He wasn't going to be that bastard, the one who took advantage when she was vulnerable. "How do you feel today? I already had River check you over, and he said you were fine, at least physically."

Just as she shrugged, her eyes finally zeroed in on his neck. She met his gaze again. "What happened to you, Stone?"

He ran his fingers over the raised flesh. Damn, he'd moved his hand when he'd taken hers. "I barely notice it anymore."

"Stone," she growled.

At her fierce tone, he fought a smile. "I had to wear a collar for ten years. Most of the time it was metal, and it chafed."

She slowly lifted a hand and then traced the scar that encircled his neck. Even though he could barely feel it, her touch sent a spark rushing through his body. "I'm not usually a violent person, but now I'm sad those bastards are already dead and I can't kill them for what they did to you."

He never wanted her to take a life and have to live with it. However, the fact his sweet, kind female would try, and for him, did something to his heart.

Stone took her hand and kissed her fingers. Only once she met his gaze again did he speak. "Then you understand what I feel about the bastards who took you, and how it's taking every bit of restraint I have not to kill them all. Slowly."

Reika snuggled closer against him. "I should be horrified at the thought of torture. And yet, I can't be. I sort of want them to suffer." She bit her lip and then searched his eyes. "Maybe I'm not as good of a person as I thought I was."

He cupped her cheek. "You are light, and sunshine, and everything good in the world, Reika Hashimoto. Maybe in your time period things are different for paranormals. But here, we mostly take care of our own criminals. And since the males who took you are part vampire and committed the crimes in their home territory, Leo will decide their punishments. I hope he makes an example out of them."

She sighed and rested her head back on his chest, wrapping her arms around him. "It's just all so weird to me. I mean, an angry cook kidnapped me for revenge." She lifted her head to prop her chin on his chest. "Is that a common thing here? Do I need to always be on high alert?"

Running the backs of his fingers down her cheek, he answered, "It's usually not that bad, no." For a beat, he hesitated about sharing what they'd discovered from the four males they'd taken prisoner. But Reika had a right to know, and Stone didn't want her hearing it from anyone else. "If not for the French vampires, the cook never would've been able to afford hiring the bastards who took you."

She searched his gaze. "What do you mean? What

French vampires? Why would they pay to have me kidnapped?"

Stone chastised himself for keeping her in the dark, but no longer. "There's bad blood between the British and French vampires." He quickly explained how the British forces had killed nearly all of the female French vampires during the Napoleonic Wars and finally added, "Now that the French have amassed significant resources again, they're bloody well bent on getting revenge. And part of their plan is funding anyone who wants to hurt Leo and our kind because it'll weaken his leadership. I also wouldn't put it past them to try and fuck up the alliance with the shifters and fae witches, and put us all at war again."

Especially since the shifters had helped the vampires during the war with the French.

She searched his gaze. "So they're pretty dangerous then. Does that mean I'm basically going to be a prisoner in one building or the other until they're dealt with?"

He shook his head. "I don't think so. Since we have four of the five males who took you—and I have people looking for the ex-cook and her niece as well—they know we'll be on high alert regarding your safety. I doubt they'd risk it when there are far easier targets." He leaned down and kissed her nose. "And I'm going to be your personal guard from now on. No one will ever steal you away again, as long as I breathe."

She raised an eyebrow. "I thought vampires couldn't lie? There's no way you can guarantee that."

"Even if I'm half—and the no lying restriction is less severe—I'm telling the truth. I will bloody well do whatever it takes to keep you from living in fear." He hesitated a beat, but then pushed on. "I want you as my bride, Reika. And I hope someday soon, you'll agree to be my wife so I can protect you with my name as well. I may be the bastard son of a whore, but my connection to Leo can help shield you."

She traced his jaw, and Stone leaned into the touch. "I don't care where you came from, Stone Riley. The male in front of me is strong, kind, and even gentle, although he hides it most of the time with scowls and grunts." He scowled deeply on purpose, and she laughed. "And you have a sense of humor dying to come out, too, I think. But…"

He brushed hair off her face. "But what?"

She moved a little until her face was nearly even with his. The gleam in her eyes made his cock come back to life. She whispered, "I think I need to try things out with a certain male, like a test drive in the bedroom department, just to make sure we're compatible."

If "test drive" meant some sort of trial, then all he wanted to do was flip Reika onto her back and show her how bloody well they'd fit. And yet, he still remembered her being shaken and terrified the day before. "I very much look forward to showing you that we are, but not until you've recovered."

She raised her chin. "I'm fine, Stone. My lady parts are in working order, and they didn't touch me, beyond tying me up. I'm not traumatized, if that's what you're worried about."

Trying not to think of Reika's cunt and how much he wanted to taste her, he focused on her face. "Right now, you probably feel obligated to me for rescuing you. But when I finally claim you, I want it to be because you want me for me."

Reika sat up and rolled her eyes. "I've wanted you pretty much since the first day we met, silly. So I guess it's up to me to get the ball rolling."

He scowled, but then she moved backward and tugged down the blanket, exposing his naked body and very hard cock laying against his stomach.

She smiled as she stared at him, and Stone resisted a groan. "What are you going to do, Reika?"

As she traced circles on his sensitive head, Stone arched his hips into her touch. He barely heard her say, "Well, I'm going to claim you first and hope you finally understand I want you for you. Then you can claim me, too."

Before he could ask what she meant—Reika wasn't a vampire, not even half, and had no need to claim— she wrapped her small, warm fingers around his cock and squeezed.

He groaned as he reveled in her touch.

Then she leaned down and flicked her tongue against the tip of him, and Stone's restraint shattered. Threading his fingers through her sleep-tousled hair, he growled, "More. I need to feel more of your mouth."

She smiled smugly up at him a beat, fire dancing in her eyes, before lowering her mouth and taking him between her lips.

And as she licked, and sucked, and tortured him

slowly, Stone groaned, and kept murmuring, "Yes, fuck, just like that."

As she continued to tease and make him lose his mind, Stone waited for the moment he could flip her onto her back and give her the best kind of revenge—with his mouth on her cunt.

Chapter Eleven

It'd been a while since Reika had gone down on a guy. She'd never really enjoyed it before, mostly because getting a guy to do the same for her had been like pulling teeth.

But with Stone, his scent, and taste, and even the way he demanded more of her, made her wetter than she'd ever been in her life.

Maybe it was because of her growing feelings for him, or how such a guarded male was allowing himself to be vulnerable with her, or a combination of the two. But making him squirm and writhe was turning her on like nothing else.

When she finally pulled back to circle his tip with her tongue, Stone growled, tossed her on her back, and spread her legs. Her grumpy half-vampire pulled up her long nightgown slowly, each inch of the material against her skin deliberate, stoking her heat and making her burn for more than the whisper of fabric.

The look in his eyes, one of reverence and fire, made her even wetter, and she ached to feel him inside her.

He most definitely looked like he wanted to devour her and wouldn't need any begging or pleading to do it.

Not for the first time, she wondered how this amazing male could possibly be real.

When he bared her pussy, he stopped and ran a finger lightly through her center. Reika arched upward and then growled when he stopped just shy of her clit. "Don't tease me like that, Stone."

He smiled—holy crap, he was even sexier when he full-blown smiled—and continued teasing her pussy with light caresses. "Didn't you say that I needed to be a bit more lighthearted and not take things as seriously?"

Stone thrust the tip of a finger inside her and then pulled away, her hips following him of their own accord.

Reika had always thought she'd enjoy more foreplay. But right here, right now, it only made her impatient. She growled. "Yeah, with jokes, or pranks, or just day-to-day life, sure. But right now, I want to feel you inside me, Stone. Don't make me beg for it."

He removed his hand and backed away. Reika nearly reached for him, but then he laid down between her legs until his head was inches from her pussy. His hot breath danced against her as he placed her knees over his shoulders. His heated gaze met hers before he replied, "Not until I make you come with my tongue. I won't last long once I bite you and taste your delicious blood for the claiming, love. So let me please you a little beforehand and get my appetizer before the main course."

As if she was going to tell him not to go down on her. She was thinking of how to taunt him a little more when he licked her slit slowly, up toward her clit and lightly stroked it.

Reika cried out and threaded her fingers into his hair.

But then Stone swirled, and licked, and suckled her clit, all while plunging two fingers inside her, and Reika lost any type of thought beyond how her reserved grump was extremely talented with his mouth.

And holy moly, he kept licking, and suckling, and bringing her to the edge but never quite sending her over. If only he'd be a little firmer with his touch. But before she could voice that, he curled his fingers in a delicious way inside her pussy, one that made her cry out and come ever closer to the fine line between pleasure and pain. Only then, as if he wanted her panting, and squirming, and ready to beg, did he finally take her bundle of nerves between his teeth, gently but hard enough to make her come.

Pleasure shot through her, spots dancing before her eyes as she cried out his name. Each pulse of her pussy, combined with Stone's mouth, tongue, and fingers still teasing her, made the waves go on and on until he finally eased his touch and let her come down.

Reika relaxed onto the bed, trying to catch her breath—because, wow, not even her best vibrator had been that good—and Stone moved to lay beside her.

His overly yummy smile returned, making her body heat up all over again.

If he ever found out his smiles made her weak and needy, she'd be doomed, but in the best way.

Stone kissed her gently before adding, "I think I just discovered my new favorite dessert."

Maybe some would think it corny, or over the top. But the blazing fire in his eyes made her pussy tingle all over again. "As long as it's not at the dinner table with others watching, I might be open to giving you dessert every night."

Stone laughed, and the sound did something to her heart. It was a bit scratchy, almost as if he hadn't done it ever before, and it was one of the most beautiful things she'd ever heard.

When he finally stopped, he took the hem of her nightgown and pulled it further up her body. "We'll have to negotiate that point." He nuzzled her cheek. "Leo's brother owns a pleasure house, and I'd like to take you there. Some of their offerings are a bit shocking, but I think my bride might like them."

She'd heard about the Victorian sex club. Although as Stone's hand slowly moved up her stomach, between her breasts, and then stopped at her upper chest to stroke her skin with his fingers, she had a hard time forming a reply. "Maybe. But I'm still waiting to see if we truly fit."

He chuckled. "Then it's time to get you naked, love. And I'll continue convincing you."

In the next instant, he had her clothes off and tossed to the ground.

Stone stared at her, his eyes lingering on her small breasts. Remembering an offhand comment from her first sexual experience at twenty, she wondered if he'd be disappointed in her size. But then he growled and took one of her nipples into his mouth, and she threaded her fingers through his hair.

Stone licked, and sucked, and nibbled, driving her crazy all over again.

She moaned, and squirmed, and opened her legs wider. However, Stone released her nipple only to move to the other. He growled, "So fucking perfect," before sweetly torturing her all over again.

Any doubts she had fled her mind. The way Stone worshiped her told her she didn't disappoint him, not even a little.

At some point he pulled back and then lightly stroked his elongated fang against her taut peak, and for the first time in her life, she wondered what it'd feel like to have a vampire bite her breast.

He kissed each breast one last time before taking her mouth with his own. She barely registered him settling between her thighs, too engrossed in the back and forth with their tongues, his taste combined with hers, and how she loved his hard, hot skin pressed up against her.

As she wrapped her arms around him and placed her hands on his back, her fingers caressed raised flesh that had to be even more scars.

But Reika was too hot, and needy, and could only think of his fangs in her neck and his dick in her pussy.

Any rational conversation, or questions, would have to wait until later.

He finally broke their kiss. "I can't hold out much longer, love. Tell me I can claim you fully now." He nuzzled her neck. "I want to feel your hot cunt wrapped around my cock as I fill you with my seed."

Oh, crap. That was right. Condoms weren't really a thing. And as much as she wanted to let him do it, she needed to try and be responsible. Stroking his back, she asked, "You, er, haven't been with tons of females, have you?"

He raised his head to meet her eyes. "No, very few. And with everyone else I've used French letters, back before I entered my frozen state."

Right, the old-timey version of a condom, according to Yesenia, made out of sheep's guts. Apparently rubber ones were still super rare. "So, you don't have any diseases?"

Full-blooded paranormals were usually immune, but if he had any human blood in him, he might not be.

He stroked her cheek. "I would never do anything to hurt you." Then he frowned. "Maybe you don't want children? I can wait until I get something from the fae witches to prevent it."

As he moved to roll away, Reika held him tightly. "No, don't go." And after studying him a beat, she added, "I want you now, Stone. Whatever happens, happens."

The way his eyes lit up told Reika that despite his

growly, loner exterior, Stone probably longed for what he'd never really had—a family.

And Reika decided right then and there she would be the one to give it to him. No matter if it ended up just her and him forever, she would be his family. Never again would Stone have to be a loner to protect himself.

She would be at his side, and they'd forge a future together, whatever that meant for two people from two very different time periods.

He asked, "Are you sure?"

She nodded. "Yeah." She arched her hips up and wriggled against his hard dick. "And you've passed the compatibility test with flying colors. So it's high time to claim me, Mr. Riley, and make me yours."

Reika nearly added "forever," but she wasn't sure if that'd be going too far.

After all, she was already in love with him, but he might not have the same feelings. While she'd been chipping away at the icy exterior, she didn't know how deep his walls might be. And yet, she hoped.

He took her lips in a slow, gentle kiss. The action tender, as if truly worshiping her, and tears nearly sprung to her eyes.

But then his rough fingers were touching her center and then her clit, and Reika forgot about everything else but how it would feel to have Stone claim her as his bride in truth.

~

Stone should say something romantic, or at least tell Reika how bloody beautiful she was, her body perfect, and her taste incredible.

But it was taking everything he had to keep his need to claim her in check. The rutting instinct of his shifter side wanted to fuck her again and again, until she was dripping cum down her leg. And his vampire side wanted her blood.

And one day he would have it all. However, this was his first time with Reika, and he wanted it to be more tender, more special, more memorable in general.

She'd already come apart on his tongue, her sweet cries music to his ears, and now she was spreading her legs, stroking his back and arching up toward him, asking Stone to make her his.

He'd find a way to tell her his feelings later. In such a short time she'd come to mean so much to him, and he would never take her for granted. Ever. Discovering that she was his fated one had made everything he'd endured worth it.

For now, he nuzzled his lips against her neck, the feel of her rapid pulse beneath his mouth making his fangs ache.

Since she would come as soon as he bit her, he would do that last. Not that it stopped him from nibbling her soft skin, or licking the sting with his tongue, or merely reveling in her fucking delicious scent.

Needing to tease her a little, he rubbed his cock up and down her center. When her nails dug into his back, he finally smiled as he positioned his cock at her entrance. "Is this what my sweet bride wants?"

Stone entered an inch and retreated. When Reika growled, he couldn't help but smile. He loved being the one who could bring out her grumpy, impatient side. "Tell me what you want, love, and I'll grant it."

She lightly scraped her nails down his back, and he fucking loved it. "Just take me, Stone. No more teasing. Just claim me and make me yours."

His fangs and cock throbbed at her words. At the desire in her eyes, he thrust until he was bollocks deep inside her. He groaned, never having felt anything so perfect before. "Fuck, Reika. The way you grip my cock."

She wriggled her hips, and Stone nearly lost his mind. "Then fuck me, Stone. I'm ready."

At her coarse language, he snarled, took her lips in a rough kiss and moved his hips.

Her tongue didn't hold back, battling his, as he continued to pump into her sweet cunny, almost as if he were addicted to her and only her.

When he finally broke the kiss, Reika closed her eyes and tilted her head, exposing her lovely, light-tanned skin up as an offering. "Bite me, Stone. I want your fangs in me. Now."

His fangs throbbed, and with a growl, he leaned down and plunged them into her flesh.

He felt her orgasm as she gripped and released him. Combined with the sweet taste of her blood on his tongue, he was close, so close. The pleasure coursing through him was almost too much.

And despite holding out for as long as he could, Stone finally stilled his hips and released inside his bride.

His vampire instinct to claim her eased. Reika was theirs, and every vampire or shifter would be able to see his bite claim on her neck.

After he'd spilled his last drop, he slowly pulled away from her neck, licked the puncture marks to seal them, and laid his forehead against her jaw. "Fuck, Reika. I never imagined you could taste so bloody good."

She stroked his back. "Well, my power is to make organic things taste better. I guess my magic must've done that to me as well."

At her teasing tone, he chuckled, rolled onto his back, and pulled Reika half over his chest. He kissed her forehead and held her close. He nearly said he loved her, but held back, not wanting to ruin the moment.

Reika finally lifted her head and met his gaze. "You're not going to pass out on me, are you?"

He resisted yawning. "Maybe. Why?"

She propped her hands on his chest and then supported her chin with them. "Because I have lots and lots of questions. And I think having you full of happy chemicals and still high from your orgasm might loosen your lips a little."

He stroked her cheek. "You're more devious than I gave you credit for." She smiled slowly, and at the sly look, he chuckled. "You are bloody marvelous, Reika

Hashimoto." And before he could think better of it, he blurted, "Will you become my bride and wife in truth? Will you marry me?"

When she blinked and remained silent, he wondered if he'd just fucked up.

Chapter Twelve

Reika was oddly energetic despite two orgasms and having her vein tapped by Stone. Her male was not in the same boat, though, as he looked about ready to fall asleep.

And yet, she didn't want to end their amazing first time together with him passing out. Not when she desperately wanted to know more about his past and the scars on his back.

Because if she could get the bad memories out of the way now, then maybe they could start planning their—hopefully—much happier future together.

Then Stone asked her to marry him. Which she wanted to do, of course. But a part of her wondered if it was just the post-orgasm bliss asking her.

His eyes shuttered, as if thinking he'd messed up, and Reika found her voice again. "I'm not saying no, Stone, but you asked me out of the blue. I just wasn't expecting it."

His expression relaxed a fraction. "So you're not trying to think of a nice way to tell me to sod off?"

She shook her head, kissed his lips gently, and then stated, "Of course not. But before I give an answer, I have a few questions."

His gaze turned wary. "Such as?"

She knew spilling even more of his heart out wouldn't be easy. He'd barely talked at all when she'd first met him, and look at how much he'd already revealed to her.

But she truly wanted to help him move past what he'd endured, and for that, he needed to tell someone about it.

To help give him some encouragement and relax a little, Reika decided to give him a nice view while asking her questions. So she straddled his hips and laid her hands on his solid, firm chest. His gaze darted to her breasts, and she felt his muscles relax under him. Just as she'd thought, boobs were a good distraction.

Just for the heck of it, she gave a little shimmy. Stone's pupils turned huge, and he growled. "Are you trying to seduce me again, love?"

Every time he said the endearment, it made her all warm and gooey inside. However, she brushed past the feeling. She was determined to clear the air about his past so they could make a bright, happy, and probably super sex-filled future. "No, just trying to relax you, and it worked. Like I said, I have some questions. Answer them, and I'll give you my answer. Hint: It's going to make you an extremely happy male."

The last traces of uneasiness faded from his gaze,

slowly replaced by pure, unadulterated joy. The sight made her throat tighten. To think she could bring so much happiness to another was still hard to swallow.

He said gruffly, "Then ask whatever you want."

"Anything? Are you sure?"

"As long as it's not permission to fuck other males, then yes."

She rolled her eyes. "Why would I do that when I have my own sexy, strong, and somewhat soft male as my own?"

"I'm not soft."

She smiled. "We can argue that point later." She sobered and leaned down so he focused on her face and not her naked torso. "Let me start with the fact I'm not trying to be cruel, or mean, or anything like that with my questions." She cupped his cheek. "I just need to know a little more about your past so I can help erase every last awful memory you have."

He searched her gaze and asked slowly, "What do you want to know?"

"How did you get the scars on your back, Stone?"

She had a feeling she knew but needed to hear it.

His eyes turned hard. "It's best if you don't know, love. Trust me."

She caressed his cheek with her thumb. "Tell me. I have a feeling this is super important, just like with your neck or even not being able to speak without permission." He didn't look convinced, so Reika added, "Nothing you say will scare me away." He remained silent, so she leaned down and brushed her lips against his. "Please tell me, Stone."

After another second, he sighed. "All right, I will. But let me sit up and hold you in my lap whilst I do it."

Not about to argue, Reika climbed off him. Stone sat against the headboard, and she sat in his lap, looping her arms around his neck. As soon as his arm came around her waist, he started talking. "I'm sure you can guess, but they were from my time with the couple who owned me."

She bobbed her head and he continued, "Well, in the beginning, I wasn't very good at listening to orders. And so when I refused to do things like suck the bastard's cock, or choke the female from behind while her husband fucked her, they started giving me lashes.

"They stung but never broke the skin in the early days. But I was stubborn back then too, and the only way they eventually got me to submit was to whip me until I bled, rubbed a special fae witch concoction into my wounds to ensure they'd never heal properly, and then threatened to do the same to every inch of my body if I didn't start following their commands."

The thought of a young Stone being whipped, let alone being used and abused by two adults, made her throat choke up and tears come to her eyes.

However, she didn't want to start crying and have Stone mistake it for pity. So she cleared her throat a few times and finally replied, "The more I learn, the more I'm glad you killed them and got away. Although a small part of me wishes I could punish them, too."

He traced her eyebrow, the bridge of her nose, and finally her lips. "Don't let them steal your inner light, love. Hurting others isn't in your nature, and I rather like my happy, energetic, and occasionally amusing witch."

She raised an eyebrow. "Occasionally amusing?" He smiled and shrugged, and the sight eased her a bit. She added, "Oh, I'm still me. But when it comes to hurting the male I love, then I want death and destruction to rain down on them."

Crap. She hadn't meant to mention love just yet.

Although as happiness glowed in Stone's eyes, his face the most relaxed she'd ever seen, hope flickered in her chest that he felt the same way.

He pulled her closer against him and he growled. "Tell me again."

Since the cat was out of the bag, she wasn't going to hold back. "I love you, Stone. Every growly, grunty, tall inch of you."

He smiled slowly. "Good because I love you too, and I'm never letting you go."

Unable to resist teasing him, she cocked an eyebrow. "I haven't officially given you my answer yet, you know."

His hand moved from her hip to her stomach and then between her thighs. Reika sucked in a breath as he brushed her clit. "Maybe you need some more convincing about our compatibility."

As he eased a finger inside her, she bit her lip to keep from moaning. "Stop. We're trying to have a serious discussion here."

"Say yes, you'll be my wife, and then we'll have our whole lives for you to pry stuff out of me."

Even as he stroked her, making her body hot and

achy all over again, she somehow managed to concentrate. "Oh, all right then. I'll marry you."

His lips crushed against hers, claiming her mouth, letting her know how much he wanted her, wanted their future, and even his joy came through.

And as he finally laid her down and thrust into her pussy again, they never severed eye contact, both of them conveying the depth of love and emotion they had for each other.

Because it didn't matter if it had been a short while, or that they were from two very different time periods in history. Reika loved Stone. She couldn't imagine being anywhere else, and she knew he'd always be at her side, loving her, supporting her, and helping to make her dreams come true.

Epilogue

Early September 1890

Stone kept a hand on Reika's lower back, guiding her inside the new building he'd bought, taking care that she didn't trip. She was, after all, wearing a blindfold and completely relying on him.

Reika, who was now his wife.

Being responsible for someone had terrified him at first. But after nearly two months of marriage, he was growing more and more used to her being at his side, and them supporting each other, no matter what.

And given how Reika's mother had declined coming to the past, Reika had definitely needed him. The only good thing was that she was able to send letters to her family, thanks to Yesenia's magic.

As he stared at his wife, her hands waving in front

of her as if searching for something, he couldn't resist leaning over and kissing her neck.

"Stop it, Stone. Just because you blindfolded me in bed a few nights ago doesn't mean I'm ready for you to take me to some random place and have your wicked way with me."

"Have I told you how much I love it when you use some of my phrases back at me?" He kissed her neck again, but this time kept her in place as he did it. "Although I think you can do a lot better than wicked."

She snorted. "Cock? Fuck? What else?" She paused and then groaned. "Please tell me we aren't somewhere public and I just made an ass out of myself."

He chuckled. "No, it's private. Just a few more steps." He helped her to the middle of the room. "Stop. Close your eyes and I'll take off the blindfold. Are they closed?"

"Yes, sir. Unlike someone, I don't cheat."

"It was only at cards, and only because I wanted to claim the bet of being able to tie you up, keep you on the edge, and then take you hard."

She blushed, and Stone focused on untying the blindfold instead of what he really wanted to do—pin her up against the wall, drink from her, and fuck her as if there was no tomorrow.

Later. His surprise would make his wife happy, and he couldn't wait to see her face.

He removed the blindfold, only to find her eyes were closed. He murmured, "Open your eyes and see your new kitchen."

She did and gasped. "Stone!" Reika quickly rushed

around the large, newly furnished kitchen, full of everything he knew she liked best.

And as she ran her hands over the unlit new cast iron range, and then the copper pots on the walls, and finally to the large sink with running water—hot and cold—her squeals got louder and louder.

Before he could blink, she dashed over and crashed against him. He instantly wrapped his arms around her. "You like it?"

When she pulled back, the excitement and joy dancing in her eyes made him want to kiss her. "Oh, so much, Stone. Is this truly mine?"

He nodded. "Not only that, but your seating area for your restaurant is through there." He waved toward one of the doors. "And our new home is upstairs."

She eyed him a beat. "So you claiming to be too busy to go look at places was a lie?"

He traced her cheek. "Not a lie, exactly. I'd already seen and found this place, but I didn't want to show it to you until I had all the upgrades done." He leaned down and whispered into her ear, "Flushing toilets, hot water, and even electric lights."

Instead of words, Reika pulled his head down so she could kiss him.

He held her even tighter as he took the kiss deeper, licking, and tasting, and letting her know with confident strokes how much he loved her.

When she finally pulled back, they both breathed heavily. "I think we should bless our new kitchen with that fantasy of yours while we still can. It'll be a health hazard later."

Since he'd told her of how he wanted to fuck her on a table in the kitchen, with Reika wearing an apron and nothing else, his cock instantly turned hard. "I don't know if there's an apron here."

Mischief danced in her eyes. "Would it be so terrible if I'm naked?"

As she started to unbutton her shirt, he growled, batted her hands aside, and undid them five times faster.

In less than a minute, his wife was naked in front of him. He kissed her, lifted her, and walked toward the large table situated in the center of the room.

Once he sat her on the edge, he spread her legs and broke the kiss. "Maybe I should have dessert first."

Her gaze burned. "I think you're right."

And so he knelt, and Stone took his time licking, lapping, and nibbling between her thighs until she screamed his name.

By the time he was inside her, had bitten her neck, and they both came, blessing the kitchen with its first set of orgasms, Stone still had trouble believing this was his life now.

However, as Reika laid her head against his shoulder and they merely held one another, murmuring words of love, Stone knew it wasn't a dream. He was happy, more than he'd ever dared to be, and all because of a sunny, amusing witch who'd appeared out of nowhere, only to end up exactly where she belonged.

With him.

∼

Turn the page for a bonus epilogue….

Bonus Epilogue

Stone watched as Nora handed the small, wrapped bundle to Reika and tried to process that he was a father now.

Reika smiled down at their baby, gently kissed his head, and then raised a hand toward Stone. "Come and meet your son, Stone."

He'd faced enemies in the heat of battle, had won an untold number of fights as a child to survive, and had even endured ten years of slavery.

However, none of those compared to the fear he felt in this moment.

Reika wiggled her fingers. "Come on. Otherwise, I'm going to name him Oscar instead of Haru."

They'd argued about names for months. Haru had been their compromise—to honor Reika's father while also having Harry as a nickname, if needed. He grunted. "He'll be teased for Oscar."

She smiled, and then he finally noticed just how

tired his wife looked—pale with dark circles under her eyes and her hair plastered to her head with sweat.

Birthing his supposedly huge child, according to River, had been hard for her.

Feeling like an arsehole, Stone sat beside his wife and kissed her forehead. "Sorry, love." He lowered his voice so that River and Nora wouldn't hear. "I'm just afraid that I'll fuck up. I don't know what to do."

She leaned against his shoulder and stared down at their son. "Neither do I. But no one will ever protect Haru better than you, so stop worrying." She looked up at him again. "Just hold him, Stone. He already wants his dad."

Taking strength from the faith in his wife's eyes, he kissed her lips and then gently lifted the tiny bundle into his arms.

While Haru had looked big in Reika's embrace, he was tiny in Stone's large hands. One wrong move, and he'd kill his son.

But then Haru squirmed, and Stone brought the babe against his chest. The slight weight and heat did something to him, and suddenly Stone knew he loved the child as much as his wife. He'd do anything and everything to protect him, not to mention give him the love and caring Stone had always wanted as a boy but had never received.

Reika put an arm around his back and with her other one, readjusted Haru's blanket. "See how easily he settled down? Haru just wanted his daddy."

For a minute or so, they merely stayed that way— Haru in his arms and Reika against his side.

The moment was one he'd never forget for the rest of his life.

Then River cleared his throat, and Stone glared at him. The fae witch put up his hands. "Sorry, but I'm not quite done with Reika. Why don't you go by the window and talk to your son while I finish up here?"

Reika moved her hand to his cheek, and Stone looked down at her. "Let River handle the afterbirth, and then we can all cuddle some more."

He grunted. "I don't cuddle."

She smiled. "Yes, you do. And you love it."

He tried not to smile and lost. He kissed Reika again. "Only with you, love. Only with you. And now our son, too."

Carefully carrying Haru to the window, Stone started telling his son what an amazing person his mother was, and how Stone would teach him everything about fighting and protecting those he loved. And no matter what ended up becoming his dominant paranormal traits—it became muddled with a child who had such a mixed parentage as Haru with a shifter, fae witch, and vampire background—he and Reika would love him forever.

All too soon Nora came to let him know that River was finished and that Reika was asking for him.

Reika yawned as Stone settled beside her. He placed their son on her chest, put an arm around Haru and her, and murmured, "Sleep, love. I'll watch over you and Haru."

She glowed as she looked at him. "I love you, Stone."

He kissed her. "I love you too, Reika."

With a smile on her face, his wife fell asleep. And Stone marveled at the miracle in his arms. Every day he didn't think he could be happier, and he yet he was constantly proven wrong. He couldn't wait to see what the future brought them next.

Author's Note

Even though this was a novella, I loved writing Stone and Reika's story so much! This story is extra special to me because I lived in Japan for four years (and yes, I even speak and read the language) and in all the years I've been writing, I haven't had a chance to use that part of my life before. I actually had to hold back on everything I wanted to include, lol. But the special New Year's dishes are real, for what it's worth. (New Year's is a huge deal in Japan.) Oh, and Reika's original hometown of Otsu is where I lived for three of those years. :) While she's fictional, she was inspired by some of the high school students I taught while living there. I have so many good memories from my time in Japan, and I hope I can use them again one day.

As for what's next, well, it will be the last Vale sibling, Meadow. She is the fated one of both Laurie and Joseph, and the three of them will make for an interesting (and hot) story. All three of them will be in a relationship with each other, so no love triangle. I hinted at it previously, but both Laurie and Joseph are bisexual, meaning swords will cross.

William Khan and Grace Black's story (*Wolf's Fae Witch Lord*) should be after that, hopefully in late 2026. There will be 7-8 books total, although I don't think any of them will be as long as River and Nora's story! (And yes, Ambrose will have a story too, eventually, and will stop making his mother sad. ;))

As always, I have a lot of people who helped me along the way. I'd like to thank:

- My betas: Iliana, Sabrina, Ash, and Mel. They catch the lingering typos or inconsistencies. These ladies are truly amazing.

- My readers and fans. You all make my dream job possible, and I couldn't do it without you!

Thanks again for reading and I can't wait to share Meadow, Laurie, and Joseph's story in *Vampires' Shared Bride*. I'll see you at the end of the next book!

About the Author

Jessie Donovan has sold over half a million books, has given away hundreds of thousands more to readers for free, and has even hit the *NY Times* and *USA Today* bestseller lists. She is best known for her dragon-shifter series, but also writes about vampires, fae witches, aliens, and even has a crazy romantic comedy series set in Scotland. When not reading a book, jogging on her treadmill, or traipsing around some foreign country on a shoestring, she can often be found interacting with her readers on Facebook or TikTok. She lives near Seattle, where, yes, it rains a lot but it also makes everything green.

Visit her website at: www.JessieDonovan.com

www.ingramcontent.com/pod-product-compliance
Lightning Source LLC
Chambersburg PA
CBHW020139180626
46810CB00004B/1645